MW01602191

Project Wormhole
Into The Unknown

Written By:
Dennis Lee Bates Jr., (Toby)

Background Cover Art:
Cody Austin Lee Bates

Disclosure:

This is a book of fiction. All characters, places and events are that of fiction. Any resemblance to actual events, locations, or persons, living or dead, is entirely coincidental. This story is not intended to teach actual historical material. Reference to historical figures or places is strictly in the sense of the story-line and plot, events and time lines may not be factual to true events as this is a work of pure fiction.

ISBN: 9798269786179

Project Wormhole
Captain's Log

It has been two hundred years since that day, that changed the universe as we know it. Nothing is the same and it never will be again. My friends, my family, they are all gone -- I am alone with just my crew and their families, who currently are in suspended animation. I alone can make the decision. Do we move forward or do I choose to terminate our mission?

Are there others out here among the stars? Did any of the others make it through? So many questions are filling my mind right now. I can't make the choice, not right now, not at this moment in time. What if I choose to wake my crew only to find that we are the last humans. A ship with only a small group of people on board trying to survive in an unknown part of the universe. I don't even know where we are. All I know, the computer initiated an emergency override to bring me out of suspended animation. The on-board computer indicates that two hundred years have passed.

But, where are we? The stars look different somehow, the galaxy is not the same. Am I still in the Milky Way? What happened to Earth? I am so confused right now. The last thing I remember was a mission to send multiple ships throughout space using a new technology that could create artificial wormholes. Something that began with the "God Particle" discovered in the early 21st century that later resulted in experiments with inter-dimensional portals and the possibility of the "multiverse". It took several years to achieve their goals, but it happened. A young physicist who had worked on the CERN program discovered what he described as a portal in the early 21st century, around the year 2045.

This was the beginning of the end. The change of the known universe was in the making and we brought it on. Did we, the human species, just start our eventual destruction?

Chapter One
The Beginning
Earth, 2045

A computerized voice was sounding an alert. "Condition red, condition red. All departments initiate emergency lockdown."

"Sir, we need to shut it down!" Shouted a voice over the sound of the alarms.

"Not yet! We have to see what this becomes, it is the discovery of a lifetime." Responded a young man dressed in a labcoat as he adjusted controls on a nearby terminal.

It was a chaotic scene as scientists and physicist from all over the world were scrambling to record this moment in time. This was sure to lead the world into new frontiers.

"Doctor!", Shouted a young lady from across the room. "We have to shut it down!"

"No, not yet! We have to --"

Suddenly the alarms stopped and things began to calm down. The events of this day were sure to be life-altering and would be one for the record books. Dr. Jean-Pierre Valentine was a world renowned physicist, a genius in his own right, who specialized in the multiverse theory. At the young age, of only 25 years old, his work had led the scientific community into a new era. It all began over fifty years ago with the official discovery of something called the 'God Particle', something that was thought to be a threat to the universe, with some believing it to be so powerful that it could in fact destroy the universe. Many wanted this experiment to end before something bad happened.

"Dr. Valentine, what are we going to do now?" Asked a young lady dressed in a lab coat. Her identification badge listed her as an assistant lab technician by the name of Sara Hart.

"I am not sure Sara, this --"

Alarms began to sound again, alerting a condition red situation calling for a lockdown. Technicians were scrambling through the lab reading off codes and data as quickly as they could.

"It's really happening." Valentine thought aloud.

"Dr. Valentine, what are we going to do now?!" Sara asked, as she shouted over the alarms from a nearby computer terminal.

"Clear the lab!" Valentine shouted.

"Sir! It's growing!" Came a voice from across the lab.

"I said clear the lab!"

Suddenly a bright light appeared inside the chamber where the experiment was taking place. Something appeared, but the young researcher knew what he was seeing was surely impossible. Years of research had now reached a pivotal point for science. A new discovery was in the making, that over the next several years would become the greatest tool in science, space exploration and perhaps more.

♦

Earth, 2085

Dr. Jean-Pierre Valentine worked quietly, alone in his lab perfecting his discovery, a discovery that could change the world. Many of his colleagues had abandoned the research, calling it too risky and a threat to humanity, but, not all of them. There were some who thought this could have potential and decided to back him in his research efforts. Sara Hart, his young lab assistant had completed her studies and was now his research partner and wife; now, Dr. Sara Hart-Valentine. The two had spent the past five years on the project that would become the most important breakthrough in the scientific community.

"This is going to change the world." Sara said as she entered the lab to assist her husband.

"You are so right my love, with this breakthrough discovery we will be able to lead the world into a new era of understanding our universe."

Just then someone arrived and both researchers quickly closed all files. As noted, not everyone was happy with this research, which brought many who would try to stop them.

"Dr. Valentine, and of course, Dr. Valentine, I presume?" A man dressed in a dark, hoodie said as he walked into the lab addressing the researchers. He was a tall man, muscular in build and spoke with an assertive tone. His face was covered, but he had a familiar appearance.

"Welcome." Jean-Pierre said, "How may I assist you?"

"It is I who can assist *you*." He began, while opening a locked case he was carrying. "This file contains instructions, follow them closely, it is in your best interest that you do so."

The mysterious man left as quickly as he came. Dr. Valentine and his wife both peered at the file left by their visitor, wondering what was so important. Slowly, they opened the folder to find a website address, with instructions to log on from a computer that was not part of the lab equipment. Sara decided it was worth the risk to use her personal computer. She entered the address and waited as the site opened up. On the screen appeared a simple message.

Do not go any further, unless you plan to go all the way.

"What?" They both questioned aloud.

"Sara, I am not sure if we should continue."

"I understand. It's up to you, but it may be worth the risk."

They both made the decision to move forward, not without caution. They chose to secure their research first, making sure that everything was safe, just in case.

"Sara, take the system off line, backup the main files. Let's make sure that all of our hard work is safe. I don't want to take any chances."

"I'm already on it my dear!"

Sara was working on the backup files while her husband and research partner worked to secure the lab. They wanted to be sure that whatever they were about to see would only be seen by them. They were still unsure as to who they were dealing with and what they wanted. They had so many questions. Jean-Pierre was working diligently as he thought back to that day when they made their discovery that made them out-casts among the science community.

♦

Earth, 2045

Dr. Valentine worked to secure the lab. The others were all unsure as to what had actually happened, but he knew. He knew what had appeared and he knew what he had to do. He had recreated an event, first confirmed in 2012 on the 4th of July, when a team of scientist confirmed evidence of the Higgs field also known as the God Particle. This time though, there was more to it.

Now, while this was viewed by many as the particle that gave all matter its mass, the fact was, it was only responsible for maybe around 1% of the mass of the human body. A fascinating discovery nonetheless. These discoveries would lead to more experiments in regards to the creation of the universe. But not everyone was as optimistic, with some giving warnings that the particle could become unstable at high energy levels, in the range of 100 billion gigaelectron volts (GeV). But this was unlikely, considering that current energy levels were not near this level, at least not at this time. Measuring at only around 100 trillion electron volts (TeV), the chances of any disaster were virtually impossible. But many were still maintaining caution.

♦

Earth, 2085

The Valentines worked quickly to secure the lab, they were about to open the site. What was about to take place was going to be life changing for the researchers and their work.

"Here goes nothing." Dr. Valentine stated as he once again entered the website.

He entered the site and again, using Sara's computer, on the screen the same warning appeared:

Do not go any further, unless you plan to go all the way.

Hesitant, he clicked on a link that simply read "continue". The screen flickered as it loaded a large file. At the top of the file the word WARNING appeared in large letters.

WARNING

The files you are about to read are TOP-SECRET and must not be shared with anyone. If you choose to continue, you are accepting all of the benefits *and* consequences associated with your work.

A flashing cursor awaited the next move from the researcher. A move that could prove to be life changing and bring possible danger. Something was about to happen and both researchers were being very cautious with their next move. Sara sat quietly as Jean-Pierre contemplated his next move. Their research, their lives were about to undergo something. But what?

"What should we do?" Sara asked as she looked over her husband's shoulder at the screen.

"I'm not sure at this point, but I fear we are about to embark on something very big and it could very well be dangerous for us both." Looking at his wife for a reassuring look, he made a decision. "Here we go, let's see what this is all about."

Dr. Valentine proceeded to the next screen, where a file slowly loaded. He could not believe what he was seeing. He and Sara just looked at each other, not sure of what to say. On the screen, was a simple phrase:

PROJECT WORMHOLE

Sara slowly sat down in the chair beside her husband, neither of them spoke a word. Only staring at the words before them. Jean-Pierre knew what it was about. His research. He had been working all these years to perfect the research from that day, the day that they had recreated the Higgs field, the God Particle. He had been working on the theories that this could open portals or lead to artificial wormholes. Thus began a long journey, one that would lead him and his wife on a life long mission to create the first artificial wormhole.

Chapter Two

TOP-SECRET MISSION

Earth, 2105

Twenty years have passed, now 85 years old, Dr. Jean-Pierre Valentine and his wife Dr. Sara Hart-Valentine, who had recently turned 83, were ready to reveal their life's work. A project that has lasted a lifetime, since that day in 2045. Now, a top-secret project that has consumed their lives was about to become reality.

"Well my love," began Jean-Pierre in a frail but stern voice. "Our life's journey has reached the climax. It is time."

"I'm so proud of you dear, this has taken so long, but the results could be monumental and can lead to so much for the world."

Time had been hard, the world has been through so much in the past sixty years. World War 3 broke out in the mid 21st century. The United States fell when the political parties split and the country was left with a president who betrayed the citizens. Now, facing civil wars, a new government had risen, a One World Government, controlled by the New United Nations. Freedom was a thing of the past. Curfews were in place around the world. Chaos was the normal. The Valentines had been working hard to develop a new tool to save humanity.

A voice came over the national communication system, calling for all citizens to report to their homes. Something was happening, something big. This only happened when the Prime Minister of the New United Nations was about to make an announcement or proclamation.

"What now?" Asked Sara as she and her husband tuned into the monitor.

A strong looking man, who appeared to be in his mid forties appeared on the monitor. Medium complected, of middle-eastern descent, he waited to begin his address. The announcer began:

"Citizens of One World Earth. All hail Prime Minister Akeem Faizan!"

"Citizens of One World Earth," The Prime Minister began. "Today marks a new era in our goals to make this planet better. Today, I bring forth a new proclamation to protect our planet from further destruction. The population of this world has led to disaster, both economic and environmental. Today, I proclaim a new order to begin immediately. We must control the population to prevent further destruction. From this day forward, no family shall have more than two children per home. Once this number has been achieved, the parents must present to the nearest medical plaza for sterilization. Furthermore, anyone over the age of sixty-five shall not be allowed to continue with function unless otherwise permitted by the New United Nations. They may choose to report to a medical plaza for end of life assistance. All medications will be disabled for anyone over the age of sixty unless otherwise permitted by the New United Nations in the interest of science and research. This proclamation shall become effective at once."

The Prime Minister ended his speech and left the stage. The Valentines stood, staring into the blank screen, they could not believe what they had just witnessed. Was the leader of the world calling for genocide? Now, the project was more important than ever. If the people of Earth have any chance of survival, without the corrupt leadership and senseless killings, they had to make this work. Now they understood what their mission was about. Survival. Freedom. Life. If this project is a success, they can save numerous lives. If it fails – life as they know it will end.

"Sara, we must see this through. We have to make a difference, without this project, I fear the end of the world is upon us."

Sara sat beside her husband, listening to his voice as tears streamed down her face, she knew what was coming. The proclamation was made and they were in that age group. Unless, for some reason, the New United Nations chose to spare their lives, they were now destined to die. She and Jean-Pierre had been married for a long time and had one son named Robert, so named after Sara's father. Robert had studied science and went on to become an astronaut with the World Space Organization.

"Jean-Pierre, what are we going to do?" Sara managed to ask her husband through her tears.

"I don't know my love, I do know that we need to complete this project now more than ever. It seems our mysterious friend who gave us this mission may have been aware of what was to come."

A knock at the door startled them both. Sara went to see who it was. She was nervous. What if it was the government there to take them in? What if they had been chosen to live? To her surprise, it was Robert.

"Mom, where is dad?" Robert asked as he entered their home.

"I'm here son, your mother and I were just listening to --"

"Dad, I know, I am here because of that. Listen, I know you have been working on a secret project. I know all about Project Wormhole. That is why I am here."

Robert had been working with a secret organization that was behind the project. They had received intelligence reports about this proclamation and knew it was coming. Project Wormhole had been put into place as a last resort to save humanity. While his parents had been working on their portion of the project, he had been working with another team of scientists who were creating a fleet of ships that would carry people off world, beyond our solar system, perhaps even into another galaxy.

"Robert, what are you talking about?" Asked Sara.

"Mom, dad, I have been a part of this project for the past five years now. In fact, I have something to tell you both."

The Valentine family sat down at the table and began to talk. Robert began to fill his parents in on the full details, including his role as the commanding officer for the lead ship.

"I want the both of you to join me on the ship."

"Son," began Jean-Pierre, "we – we can't. We have a mission here, we knew there would be a ship, however, we did not know it was this. We have to remain here --"

"No dad, please, there has to be a way --"

"Robert, please listen. We all have a mission to save humanity from destruction, our part is to make sure the wormhole opens as planned. Now, we have worked out details for one ship, and now we know which one, to carry a similar device on board."

Jean-Pierre took his son to the lab and showed him the project and how it would work. He also prepared the portable generator for him to take onto his ship and how to integrate it into the ship systems.

"Dad, this will work, I know it will. We can transport a fleet of ships using this device, once we establish a colony, we can send more ships back to gather more."

"Son, once we activate the wormhole generator the ships will have only a short amount of time to enter, once they all enter, the system will automatically self destruct to prevent the device from falling into the wrong hands. Your mother and I love you, but you have to understand. Our place is here."

The three sat quietly for what seemed like hours, in reality only about a half hour had passed. They made preparations of how things would go. Jean-Pierre and Sara would engage the device remotely through a satellite link up. At that time, Robert would lead the ships through. Each ship would carry a crew of at least one hundred and a civilian complement of approximately one hundred consisting of volunteers and the crew families. All but the commanding officers would enter into a state of suspended animation or stasis. Once the ships were in the worm-hole and on course the commanding officers would then enter stasis. At this point the onboard computer would take over, and wake the crew once a habitable planet was located. It could take a very long time. Each ship was able to sustain the life of the crew and families for as long as needed, with each ship being powered by a state-of-the-art computer system that could gener-ate power using the very technology that gave the world access to wormholes.

"Mom, dad. I understand that you must remain here. It is truly going to be hard, knowing that you are here with -- well, with all of this that is going on. One day, we will find a way to set things right in this world. Maybe, just maybe, we can find a way to help future generations."

An alarm sounded, the program was ready. It was time. Robert received a call from the mission command center, hidden deep in the valleys of the mid-west of the former United States of America, now simply known as the North American Region. The United States was no more. No more Canada, Mexico, or any other nation that was a separate government. All nations were now united under the New United Nations. The countries of Central and South America were now under the same leader. If you can call him a leader. This was more of a ruler, someone who was determined to rule the world as some supreme leader.

It was time. The fleet was ready and all ships had been boarded with all passengers safely in their stasis units where they would spend the entire trip in suspended animation. Each com-manding officer would maintain control while the ships entered into the wormhole. At that point, they would join the others in stasis.

"It's time." Jean-Pierre stated as he and Sara gave their son a final hug, sending him on his mission to help save the world.

"Mom, take care of dad. I know we are doing the right thing, but I am going to miss you both." Robert gave one last hug as he left to join his crew.

"Sara, we have to start the program." Announced Jean-Pierre as he began a countdown process on the lab computer.

An automated voice announced a countdown sequence of thirty minutes to project initiation. The Valentines would have only a few seconds to terminate the mission if something went wrong. Sara watched the monitor as she fought back tears, knowing that was the last time she would see her son. Robert had a private shuttle, somewhat new technology, waiting to take him to the launch area. Only about fifteen minutes away with the help of the shuttle.

Chapter Three
Through The Wormhole
Earth, 2105

Robert had boarded and the final countdown status began.

"T-Minus ten minutes until wormhole activation," announced the computer.

"This is Captain Robert Valentine of the U.S.S. Jean-Pierre to all fleet ships. Prepare for launch sequence." Robert was quickly switching between monitors on the bridge of his ship, named after his father. The computer continuing the count-down, now at eight minutes in.

"Captain Valentine, this is Fleet Command, you are clear for lift off."

"Copy that command. Attention fleet, engage engines at full thrust. Be alert as I am sure the military will attempt to stop us."

The fleet began their ascent as Jean-Pierre and Sara began the activation of the wormhole. Robert in the lead ship, guided the fleet ahead. Just as they were expecting, the military was on alert and trying to stop them. Thankfully each ship was equipped with the latest technology in shielding and weapons. The mission team decided it was best that each ship be equipped with this in the off chance of encountering hostile life.

"Captain Valentine, you have an incoming message." Alert-ed the onboard computer.

"Robert, your mother and I have faith that this mission will be a success. Godspeed to you and your fleet." Announced his father who was then joined by Sara as they spoke in unison to their son; "We love you Robert Valentine."

Communications went silent as the fleet began to approach the event horizon of the wormhole that was now open. With the Jean-Pierre in lead, they entered one by one into the unknown.

"Dr. Valentine," began a voice from mission command. "We have success! It appears the entire fleet has safely crossed the event horizon. We should have satellite contact in the next few days from our deep space satellite feed."

Sara was emotional as she witnessed her only son cross into the unknown. Jean-Pierre comforted his wife, as they watched their son vanish into the wormhole and now awaited their own unknown future. They were sure that government officials would be coming soon, there was no way this mission wasn't witnessed by someone high up.

"Sara," her husband began in a solemn tone. "You know what we have to do. We cannot allow this research to fall into the wrong hands. We must destroy it all."

With tears in her eyes, Sara responded. "I understand, one day, we will all be together again."

◆

An Unknown Part of Space

The Jean-Pierre was now operating under the control of onboard computer systems. Captain Valentine had entered into his stasis unit for the long journey, that could take several years. Each ship within the fleet was now fully automated and would continue to travel at speeds reaching approximately 200,000 kph. Each ship would take a separate course in order to better their chances of locating a planet capable of sustaining life, at which point the computer would then bring the captain out of stasis in order to confirm the finding and to attempt communications with any potential life on that planet. It was estimated that this could take up to ten years to achieve. The suspended animation units could sustain life indefinitely as long as the ship had power.

◆

Earth, 2105

The Valentines had destroyed the files and everything that was involved with Project Wormhole. Their plans were to move to a nice quiet place and live out their lives away from all of the chaos in the world. Although they were up in age, both were healthy.

"Sara, are you sorry that we destroyed everything?" Asked Jean-Pierre as he loaded their personal items into their transport.

"Of course not, we knew it had to be done, to protect Robert and the others. We knew this was coming."

Just as they were about to leave, a message came across from mission command for the wormhole team, it was the same man who had started this whole thing.

"Dr. Valentine, you are not leaving already are you?" He asked in that same intimidating tone.

"Well, the mission was a success, Sara and I feel our work here is done."

"Oh no my friend, your work has just begun." His tone was now deeper and seemed more sinister than before.

"What do you mean?" Sara asked.

"Trust me, you will soon find out. You see, the Prime Minister has plans for the two of you."

"Wait, I thought you were with the underground movement!" Jean-Pierre exclaimed in protest. "What is this all about?"

Jean-Pierre was upset as his wife tried to calm him. What was going on? Why the sudden change?

"That was just to get your son out of the way! He and all of his anti-government groups were becoming a threat to everything. Trust me, we have much higher plans for Project Wormhole."

"You're too late!" Sara exclaimed, "We destroyed everything."

"Oh, I don't think the good doctor here *really* destroyed it all. This has been his life long passion to see what this could become. Isn't that right, Jean-Pierre?"

"Not this time. The files are all gone. I am too old to keep going with this, I want to live out the rest of my life with my wife. I am finished with research. Besides, there is nothing more that can come of this research, not in my lifetime at least."

"You fool! You have just signed your own death warrant for both you and your wife! This could have made a difference in the world. You don't understand what you have done!"

With that, their unwanted guest signed off, ending his transmission. Sara began to cry as Jean-Pierre held her close.

"Sara, we have to go, now."

"What is it?"

"Don't say anything more, I don't want to talk about this any longer, let's just go. Now."

The Valentines loaded into their transport and headed off to one of many remote islands they owned in the Pacific, located in what was once considered international waters, but now, under this One World government, things were uncertain for them. It took them around two hours to reach their destination, at which point, Jean-Pierre set the autopilot to send the transport into the ocean. His plan was to make it appear they had crashed and drowned.

"Jean-Pierre, what is going on?" Sara asked as they made camp for the evening.

"I don't want to talk about it right now."

"What is going on?"

"I said I don't want to talk about it! Look, I -- I am sorry my love, there is just so much right now -- too much to explain."

◆

New United Nations, 2105

"How could you let this happen?!" Prime Minister Faizan exclaimed as he questioned the stranger who had been behind all of this.

"I am sorry Mr. Prime Minister sir. I never expected them to destroy the files, in fact, we figured Valentine would have already been working on a way to expand the wormhole himself as a way to gain access to his son."

"Do you really think he would destroy his life's work you imbecile!? Of course he didn't! I can assure you, he has a backup copy of the file and where ever he and his wife have disappeared to, they have it with them and I would say he has a remote lab somewhere."

"I'm on it sir. If it is there, we will find it."

"You better, if these two cause any problems with my plans, it will be on your head, or perhaps your head on the chopping block!"

"I understand sir, I will find them."

"By the way, I like to know who I am dealing with and up until now, it didn't matter. What is your name soldier?"

"My name sir?"

"Yes, you know the name your mother gave you at birth? What is it!?"

"I -- well sir, I am Lieutenant Sims of the Special Forces Division. Proudly I am serving the One World Movement and the New United Nations."

"Well Sims, if you want to keep that title, or perhaps even move higher in rank, I suggest you get me results! Now, move!!"

"Yes, Mr. Prime Minister, sir. I am on my way and I will not disappoint you. I am pretty sure I know --"

"Silence! Just get me results and I want them within the next week, before my next big proclamation. Without that file, we cannot move forward and our movement will be in danger. I will not fail!"

Sims, feeling uncertain of things now, made plans to reach out to the Valentines. There was something about Faizan, maybe something that he said that he just could not get past. There was something he was now feeling, something he should know. Perhaps it will come to him.

Chapter Four
Remote Island and Hidden Labs
Earth, 2105

The Valentines had made camp for the night, at first light they would make their way to their hidden lab. The lab was originally used by Jean-Pierre when he first discovered the stable particle. A completely self-contained lab with solar power and a link up to a private satellite system, the perfect place to continue his work.

"What are you doing?" Sara asked as she was preparing a pot of tea and some sandwiches from their pack.

"Nothing my love, I was just checking some notes." He replied as he quickly put away a notebook he was looking over.

"You know," Sara began, "I know Robert is going to be okay, he helped to create that fleet of ships. He is an intelligent man who knows as much about physics as you."

"More my love, more -- Robert is one of the brightest minds I know --" He paused, looking off into the heavens.

"What is it? What's wrong?"

"Oh nothing, I was just looking, wondering, which part of our vast galaxy or further did they end up in."

"Come on dear, let's eat and get some rest. We can head to our new home at sunrise."

"I'm not really hungry, I think I'm going to just lay here and look at the stars. You know, he's out there and he is working to save humanity, I know his mission will be a success."

They both decided to just have some tea and watch the stars. Morning would come soon enough and they had a lot of work to do in order to make this their new home. Jean-Pierre would continue his research, it was his life's passion and he knew he had a lot to carry on. His research could lead to a lot, including ways to solve the world's energy problems. Only if --

♦

New United Nations, 2105

Prime Minister Faizan paced back and forth in front of the bay window of his office, glaring at the night sky. He knew something was wrong, his plan was not going as it should. Two key people had outsmarted his move to stop them. A movement was taking place in the world, there was talk of an uprising to stop the One World government.

"Get me Lieutenant Sims!" He called out to his assistant

Faizan sat at his desk as he thumbed through a notebook, his eyes locked onto a page. "How could I have missed this?" He thought aloud.

"Mr. Prime Minister, sir, you called for me?"

"Ah, Sims, yes. I was just wondering, how exactly our friends were able to get away so easily, and I was curious as to whether you may have any suggestions?"

"Sir, I am not sure what happened. Dr. Valentine is intelligent and quite capable. Perhaps, he was suspicious all along of me and had a contingency plan in place."

"Or perhaps, he was assisted in some way or by someone. What exactly did you do to try stopping him?"

"Sir?"

"You heard me! There is no reason two old people should be able to escape from a trained soldier!"

"If you are saying that I helped them to escape in some way, I take extreme offense to that assumption. Moreover, sir, I am not one to be falsely accused, I would suggest you consider that."

Sims walked out the office leaving behind a very angry leader who was now cursing very loudly.

"Sims! I am not finished with you!"

With that, he stopped and turned slowly to face Faizan. Sims spoke with a strong and calm voice: "Sir, I promise, you will not like me very much, especially if you continue shouting at me. I strongly suggest you change your tone."

Sims was a tall, burly and well spoken soldier. When he spoke, he presented with extreme clarity and assertiveness. His voice demanded attention.

"How dare you threaten me!"

"Threaten you?" Sims laughed. "*You* are not worth my time. Now, I am leaving, *if* that is okay with you. Sir."

"Just find them and take care of this!"

"Very well, sir."

◆

Valentine Island

Earth, 2105

"Sara, I am sorry that we must live this way now, away from everyone."

"No, there is no need to be sorry, we had no choice. Things are crazy in the world now, so many lives are in danger."

"Well, this island will give us everything we need. We have a garden with a seed vault that has enough seeds to sustain us with vegetables and we have other vegetation on the island. We are completely self contained and with access to our own satellites we can continue with our work."

"I just can't believe we were set up. Mr. Sims seemed so nice."

"I know my love, I should have been more cautious. I should have noticed something was off."

"There is a message coming across. You're not going to believe this. It is him, it's Sims!"

Please, allow me to help you. I know the last person you would expect to hear from would be me, but I was truly unaware as to the plans that Faizan had until he made his proclamation. I know you are hidden away somewhere and I do not expect you to trust me, as you should not. If you will give me a chance, I think I can offer you some assistance that could prove invaluable in your work. I truly did not know.

"What is going on?" Sara asked.

"I honestly do not know what to think. He betrayed us once, however, he may have access to information we may need."

"What happened? Why is the government so interested in your work?"

"I really don't want to talk about it right now."

"Why? What did you do? There is something you are not telling me!"

"Sara, I promise I will tell you everything, but right now we need to focus on this."

Sara began to cry as she sat quietly by her husband.

"Sara, listen, I am sorry this is all happening. I promise, you will understand. Please, don't cry my love."

"What are you hiding?"

"Nothing, not exactly. I -- I had no choice."

"No choice?"

Jean-Pierre was silent for a moment before responding.

"Do you remember the day we discovered the stable version of the God Particle?"

"Yes, I remember."

"Well, there was more. The particle became unstable during the second experiment, in the process – I still cannot believe what I saw that day. I was alone in the lab when the particle became unstable, I was thinking it would just phase out. It did not. In fact, just the opposite. Something began to happen, a -- a portal of some sort began to appear."

"What? Why didn't you tell me?"

"There is more. I panicked. I shut the experiment down, or so I thought. I left the lab, only to come back --" He paused.

"What? What did you see?"

"Well, the portal was there again. This time, it was stable and remaining open. I went to shut off the system and --"

"What? What happened?" Sara asked emphatically.

"A figure emerged from the portal, for a brief moment. It appeared to be a man. I assumed, that perhaps, he had appeared from another universe. However, I was wrong."

"Where was he from?"

"Another planet." Jean-Pierre whispered. "Sara, I had no idea. Our friend Sims -- he is that man."

"What?! Sims is an alien?"

"Not exactly, he is human, it is hard to explain. You see, this portal opened to a different time. He is from another planet, in the future."

"Time travel? I thought that was impossible."

"Apparently not. The portal opened a link to the year 2345, where Sims is from. Humans have colonized, or will colonize, other planets by then. At least that is what I understand."

"So, is Sims a descendant of someone from the fleet?"

"Yes."

"How did you find out?"

"After that first appearance, he appeared again while I was working in the lab, alone. He then began to tell me everything that he felt was important to the mission. Sara, I never wanted to lie to you, but he said the safety of our family depended on his identity being kept secret. He didn't even tell me everything, not at first. In fact, this entire wormhole project was something I knew nothing about."

"And that is why you have been so quiet since all of this happened." Sara said in a comforting tone to her husband.

"Yes, partly. I never imagined that he was working with the New United Nations and Faizan. At least not considering --"

He stopped, looking through the window in their new home, looking out to the stars.

"Considering what? You know who he is don't you. You know who his family is."

"That is what is so bothersome to me. Because of who he is and I – I don't understand why he has done this. We knew what the mission was about. I just do not understand why he did this."

"Who is he?" Sara asked.

"He's – our grandson."

"What?!"

"He is Robert's son, from the future."

"Why did you keep this from me? Why did he do this?"

"I don't know why he was working with Faizan, perhaps there is more than we realize at stake here. He has asked to talk to us, perhaps we should give him a chance."

"What I don't understand is, why he is using the name Sims."

"Because giving his real name would reveal who he is --" Jean-Pierre paused briefly "If he revealed to everyone that he was from the future and that he was our grandson, it could have led to the end of the project and possibly the end of life as we all know it. Faizan has but one thing on his mind and that is world domination. He has to be stopped."

"What are you going to do? Are you meeting with him?"

"Sara, this could all be a trap, but – he is our grandson, we need to give him a chance to prove himself to us. Email him back, tell him we will talk. I will arrange to bring him here, but on my terms."

Sara sent an email to Sims, giving the instructions and where to wait for transportation to the island. Jean-Pierre owned a few things that could be helpful in their work, including a heli-copter. He would pick up his grandson at a remote location, pro-vide him with a safe sedative while transporting to the island. That was the plan as of now.

"Do you really think this is wise?" Sara asked as she prepared the sedative.

"It is our only option, we have to find out what is going on. I have to know, I have to."

"I understand, but – please, be careful. Keep in mind, he is from the future and we don't know what happened after the fleet left here."

"We can only imagine, my love, we can only imagine. It had to be an ordeal for them all, starting new lives, new civilizations. It – all seems weird, I mean how could they have started new lives so fast? And why so far into the future?"

"Robert was a very intelligent man, after all, he is his father's son. I am sure he did amazing things."

Both researchers sat, looking out at the sky, knowing that their son was somewhere out there among the stars. Starting a new family, helping to build new civilizations and colonizing other planets.

"Sara, I know things seem strange right now, but we have to be careful, not just of our visitor but of changing history."

"What do you mean?"

"Time travel has always been a topic of interest in the science communities. However, one concern, a big concern, is that of changing history. What impact it could have on future events, even lives of others. Changing one thing could set forth a vast chain of events that could have catastrophic consequences. But, it is a risk we must take. I am sure, if Robert has anything to do with this, that he has prepared his son for the mission. And, I am sure he had a good reason to send him back."

"I know exactly what you are talking about. A paradox event, and that is something we need to be aware of." Sara said.

"That's right my love, I forget sometimes that temporal studies was a side project of yours."

Chapter Five

Family Reunion or Family Preunion?

Earth, 2105

The helicopter landed and Jean-Pierre waited for his guest to arrive. He knew things were about to get even more complex. Now that Sara knew who he really was, they had a lot of questions. Why did he return? What happened to the fleet? There was just so much that they needed answers for.

"Dr. Valentine, thank you for giving me the opportunity to meet with you."

"Drop the act Sims. Or would you prefer I call you grandson?"

"Ah, yes, well we will talk more about that later. You know, in private."

"We have prepared a sedative, for precautionary measures, for transporting you to the island. We must maintain its secrecy."

"I understand, however, be warned, your sedative may not work on me. My metabolism is much better than the average man. It may require a stronger dose."

"Okay, how much stronger?"

"I would suggest you double the dose, to start."

"Perhaps we should try something else. Would you consider blindfolding and allowing me to tie your hands and feet?"

"You may do so, if you so choose. But know this, I am a very strong man and can easily break free of simple ropes. I would suggest using something much stronger."

"Well, I have some chain in the storage compartment."

"Very well, that should suffice."

Valentine blindfolded his guest first, then bound his hands and feet with the chain. They lifted off and headed towards the island, which would be a short trip, only about thirty minutes.

While it was quiet for the first five minutes or so, Sims broke the silence.

"Dr. Valentine, as I am sure you are well aware by now, my name is not Sims. At least not originally. I assumed this name for my mission. As I told you from the first time we met. I am Robert Valentine's son and I come from the future, thanks to you and your discovery. With that said, you may call me Frank."

"Frank Valentine. I like that."

"Yes, my mother chose that name."

"I would like to hear more about your family. But, for now, we are arriving at our destination. We will be changing transportation here, moving to a small boat."

"You mean we are not at your island?"

"No, as a security measure, I chose to move through a few stops along the way."

"You are smarter than I first believed. Well played. Well played indeed."

They boarded the small boat and made their way to another small island, where they would again switch to another form of transportation. The plan was to leave anyone who may be tracing their moves confused. The helicopter pad was linked to an underground facility, where it would be stored out of sight, in fact, the small island would appear to be deserted. The next island was another small island where the boat could be hidden in a nearby cave. They would then take a small two person canoe the final distance.

"So, tell me, why all of the islands?"

"You don't spend your entire adult life working on projects that many people find dangerous without a place of refuge."

"Indeed." Frank responded with admiration.

"You are not a man of many words are you Frank?"

"In my line of work, I do not talk to many people."

"That is too bad, I would imagine you have a lot to say, to someone who would listen. We have arrived. You will remain blindfolded and your hands bound until we reach our destination, however, I will release your legs as we will be traveling on foot the remainder of the way."

Seriously? He is taking this secrecy to an all time high. Frank thought.

They continued on their way, without talking too much along the way. The journey wouldn't take that long, as they were only traveling a little less than a kilometer. Once they arrive at the lab, they would handle their meeting in a secured area. Sara had been working to secure all of their work and placing hard copies in a vault.

"We are here." Jean-Pierre stated as he escorted Frank into the secured area, he then removed his blind fold and chains. "Please wait here, Sara and I will return shortly."

"I understand," Frank responded as he massaged his wrists from wearing the chains for so long and allowed his vision to adjust from the darkness. "I hope we can work together on this."

"We shall see, please wait here."

With that, he left Frank in a locked room and hurried to help Sara as she prepared them all tea and sandwiches. She wanted to make their meeting as smooth as possible.

"We are ready," Jean-Pierre announced to his wife. "I think he is going to be helpful."

Sara had been waiting in their kitchen, a much smaller area than that they left behind.

"Where is Sims?" She asked. "Do you think it was wise to leave him unattended?"

"He will be fine, I have him locked in the old conference area, he can't access anything from there."

"What have you learned so far from him?"

He thought for a moment on how to tell his wife everything.

"First of all, his name of course is not Sims, it is Frank. So far, that is all I have on him. He has been cooperative -- so far."

"Well, I guess we will find out soon." Sara said as they made their way to where their guest was waiting.

"Be careful," Jean-Pierre whispered as they approached the door. "He is a clever individual and powerful."

Frank sat patiently waiting and thinking. *I know this is going to be hard for them to comprehend. I needed Faizan to believe I was working with him in order for everything to work.*

"Hello Frank," Jean-Pierre said as they entered the room. "I hope we didn't keep you waiting too long."

"Not at all, it allowed time for me to clear my mind."

"I hope you like tea and turkey sandwiches." Sara said as she handed him a plate with a sandwich, some pickles and a tall glass of iced tea.

"Yes, that sounds good," Frank said then took a bite of his sandwich. "That is delicious. I don't get *real* meat in my time. I know you two have a lot on your mind and seek answers."

"We sure do." Sara said.

"Let us begin with some basics," Jean-Pierre said, he then took a sip of his tea and continued. "When you first arrived, you said you could help us, then you left us with a computer file that led to our current situation."

"Ah yes, the Project Wormhole file." Frank said. "This was not my file, in fact, it really was your own discovery. I just made a few changes along the way."

"Changes?" Jean-Pierre asked.

"There are some things that happened, or rather, that will happen --" He paused, thinking of the proper way to handle this apparent paradox. "Let me explain. First of all, what I am about to share with you may be disturbing, perhaps your wife should give us a little time alone, then you can give her details as you feel best for her."

"Sara," Jean-Pierre said. "If you don't mind, could you wait in the family room?"

"Sure, please be careful though."

Sara made her way out while Frank continued to tell his story or at least try to give some details as to the events that led to where they are now.

"Please continue Frank."

"As I said, the project is yours. You would have discovered a stable wormhole sometime next year. However, that discovery brought forth or would have brought forth a chain of events far worse than what we have seen so far."

"I'm listening."

"Things went, or will, or rather would have, went differently. Robert, my father, would still command the fleet but for a completely different mission. One that will go horribly wrong."

"Well, he apparently survived, considering you are here."

"Indeed. However, many of the ships were damaged and the crews lost. This event may or may not take place now, because I have already set forth some changes."

"A paradox." Jean-Pierre added.

"Not entirely. You see, changes have been set forth, however, those changes may or may not bring forth a major historical change. Meaning, that only the time frame of certain events have been changed, not the events themselves. Allow me to give an example; you would have made this discovery on your own and my father would have commanded the fleet. The only change in this is that the events have taken place a year sooner."

"I am not sure I understand, if there are no significant changes, why have you come back?"

"That is the one major change. Not one that will affect my mission as a whole, as in a danger to my time-line, however, my mission thus far has saved your life and your wife's life."

"So, if no major changes, then what was the point?"

"To get my father and his fleet through the wormhole sooner and to try to fix the mistake."

"What mistake?"

Frank hesitated before answering. "Most of my father's fleet arrived through the wormhole with no issues, however, there were some casualties. He lost two of his best ships."

"That explains part of this mission, but there is one thing I do not understand and you have never hinted to the answer. This has puzzled me from the start of this. How are you my grandson, yet you are from over two hundred years in the future?"

"That is one of the issues we hope to fix." Frank paused as he looked deep into his grandfather's eyes. "I see a lot of my father in your eyes. Most of the fleet was trapped in some type of event horizon on the opposite side of the wormhole. While time passed normally for others it became very slow for the remainder of the fleet. Once the ships broke free, they found themselves in the future by two hundred years."

"Then what is the issue? The mission, for the most part, was a success." Jean-Pierre said, as he finished off the last bite of his sandwich. "It seems that everything went well, he apparently had a family."

"Yes, this is true. However, I don't feel that the time-line has reset."

"This is a job for Sara, let me get her back in here."

Frank sat thinking once more, while waiting on Sara to join them. While he had changed history, he wondered if he changed enough of history to make a difference. Did he go far enough back in time? Should he had given his father a message, to warn him of what was to come?

"Hello Frank," Sara said. "I understand there seems to be a possible time paradox concern."

Frank thought before responding. How much should he reveal and what could it do to the time-lines?

"Indeed." Frank said. "I am uncertain if my actions have made a difference in the time-line, other than saving your lives. That was a positive result."

"I see, well, Jean-Pierre has given me some details and from what I understand your original mission was to influence the outcome of the fleet's mission. Correct?"

"Yes, that was the expected outcome of my mission. However, Prime Minister Faizan became an issue when he implemented his proclamation when he did. That was a change of events I was not expecting."

"I don't understand." Jean-Pierre said. "How was that a change of events?"

"His proclamation to limit the population size was not in the plans, at least not this soon. I have yet to determine how my being here could possibly have changed that. I have done nothing that should have affected the time-line in that manner."

"Perhaps," Sara said, "it was not you."

"Explain this thought process." Frank said, with a raised brow as he sat up straight to hear her explanation.

"Hear me out. The events that have led to this day began with your arrival, including the early creation of the fleet. Correct?"

"Yes, this is correct."

"Now, when you first arrived and met Jean-Pierre, that set us into a chain of events. The question is, what happened to make things go as it did?"

Sara thought for moment, while her husband and grandson talked quietly about the mission and how the fleet progressed. Frank had some thoughts himself on the matter, but waited on Sara as she sat quietly thinking about the events and apparent changes.

"I think I have an answer." Sara said after several minutes. "I think I know what happened. In this time-line and in yours. The answer is the fleet itself. There had to be saboteur on board one of the ships and someone on the inside who worked with Faizan."

"That is an intriguing thought," Frank said. "One that has a lot of merit and, it would not alter the time-line in any major ways, other than the fact it saved your lives. The only difference is, the events took place one year earlier."

"That leaves to question then," Jean-Pierre said. "Why are you still here? What happened to Robert and the fleet?"

"I do not know. I do know this, Faizan will not stop until he finds you. The plan was to return to this time, in hopes that by sending the fleet out earlier, perhaps a change would take place. It appears that did not happen."

"The fact you are still here means that Robert survived, if he had not, the time-line would have reset and you would not be here." Sara said. "I am going to check something, you two have some more tea."

Sara made her way to the main lab, she had a thought, it was possible things have changed only slightly. If the time-line didn't change, at least not as they could see now, perhaps the future time-line is still moving forward without any major change.

"Wait, something is not right." Frank said as he stood abruptly.

"What is it?" Jean-Pierre asked.

"This, I am not sure. Something is different."

"Can you explain?"

"No. No I cannot. It -- it seems I have, I feel as if I have --"

"Frank, what is it?"

"This is not right, we should not be here. I cannot explain it, but I just know. Something went or rather will go wrong."

"Take it easy Frank, perhaps this is a side effect of time travel. Let me get Sara in here."

"No!"

"Frank, what is it?"

"I have to go back, something is wrong!

Frank was becoming more agitated. He knew he had to get out of there, but he didn't know why. Something was bothering him and he couldn't shake the feeling he was having. Something had went wrong in the time-line, but where and what was it? Other than sending the fleet out a year early and the events with Faizan, he could not understand what he was feeling.

Sara worked to determine what changes had taken place, if any, that could be considered major event changes. Was it something that involved the fleet? Was it involving Faizan and the events of the One World Government? She too knew something was not right with her grandson. She could see the distress building within and his connection to the future definitely was part of that feeling he was having.

Sara continued to work as she thought to herself. *What if by sending the fleet ahead one year early affected the time-line somehow?* She continued her research, looking for anything that could explain the current events.

Frank, in the meantime, continued to get more anxious, more agitated at the feelings he was having. He was now more certain that something had changed with the time-lines, he just wasn't sure if it was from his time or the current time.

What if my actions have destroyed lives in the future? He thought to himself. Becoming more convinced that a major change has taken place. But what was that change? Was it something that would affect his parents or his friends? Was this his fault or was there someone else involved? *I have to return now. This has to be corrected.*

"This is impossible to figure out!" Sara exclaimed. She was determined to find an answer to the changes. Something had to be there, but what was it? Was it so simple she was overlooking it or was it much bigger?

This is why man should never play with time travel. She thought, as she kept looking, looking for even the smallest thing that could be different. There was only one problem. She had no idea what she was looking for. If there was a change, how would she know what it was? If the change was in the future, she would never be able to find it. What if her searching was the change? What if keeping Frank there was the change? This was the problem with time travel and the risk of paradoxes. The slightest thing could cause such a ripple in time it could affect everything.

Chapter Six
Universal Connections

Somewhere in the Milky Way, Earth Year 2305

Captain Robert Valentine silenced the alarms. According to the computer, they were somewhere in the Milky Way Galaxy, now he needed to pull star maps to determine an exact location.

"Computer, initiate scans to determine the current location and display on main viewer."

This is amazing. I can't believe the worm hole took us this far from home.

The ship's internal chronometer displayed two hundred years had passed. Captain Valentine entered all of this into his log and continued his mission.

"Computer, scan for other ships and awaken the first officer."

He continued monitoring for other ships, he also initiated a distress beacon. At this point, he was unsure if any of the others survived or not. His first officer was now the only other crew member awake, for the moment; she had just completed an automated medical scan in the medical bay.

"Commander Jillian Wright reporting for duty sir."

A tall woman with dark brown hair walked onto the bridge, wearing a blue uniform with a patch bearing the name of their ship; U.S.S. Jean-Pierre.

"Welcome to the bridge commander."

"Sir," she said, looking around. "Why are we the only two crew members that have been awakened?"

"Take a look." Robert said, as he pointed to the main view screen. "Welcome, commander, to the Alpha Centauri system. Oh, did I mention, that according to the chronometer, we are now two hundred years in the future? At least as far as earth time."

"Is it possible we traveled in time two hundred years?"

"Honestly? I do not know. There could be some issues with the chronometer, or perhaps the wormhole created some type of rip in the fabric of space and time."

"We should wake the others."

"Not yet commander, we need to talk."

"Sir?"

"As of now, I can't locate any other ships in our fleet and we have no idea if Alpha Centauri is a habitable system."

"Captain, are you suggesting that we terminate our mission?"

"All I know is this," Robert said. "It appears at this time we are alone in the galaxy and far from home. I will continue to scan for other ships."

"Captain, I know it seems we are alone, but we have a full crew and civilians on board."

"True, however, it is only a small number; only two hundred."

"Sir! I am picking up a signal, it is coming from a planet near Proxima Centauri. It appears to be coming from Proxima b."

"Good work commander! Computer, set course for the planet Proxima b."

With the ship operating almost entirely on automation, Robert and his first officer made their way to the stasis chambers where they chose to awaken the crew. They would manually override the suspended animation units.

"Captain --"

"Please, we are a long way from home and we will be working together for a long while. Call me Robert."

"Call me Jillian, or Jill." She said. "Robert, what if the signal proves to be something else?"

"It could very well be, but we have to find out and you are right, we're going to need a crew."

They worked to awaken everyone and let them all know what they would be facing. While some were visibly concerned, they were all more than willing to do their part in finding answers. Their hope was to find the other ships and to find a planet capable of sustaining human life. Would they meet other life? They had so many unanswered questions.

"Jill, give me ship wide communications."

"Aye sir, ship wide."

"Now here this." Robert said as he addressed his crew. "We are a long way from home and at this time we have lost contact with the rest of our fleet. A signal has been detected coming from a planet here in the Alpha Centauri system. We are in route to Proxima b, where we have determined the signal has originated. I will not lie, we will be facing the unknown. There is a strong possibility that we are the only members of our fleet, the only humans left. I know you are concerned, perhaps even afraid of what we might find. Know this, I and my first officer are here for each and everyone of you, and together, we will survive this. Now, I need all senior officers to report to the bridge."

Robert completed his announcement, now he had to get his new crew ready for their first mission.

"Okay Jill, we have a lot to prepare for. We don't know how many ships, if any, of our fleet survived. There is a signal that is coming from Proxima b indicating life, of some type."

"It is possible that the signal is an automated distress from a crashed ship. I should be getting a better fix on it momentarily."

Senior officers arrived to their stations and began working to determine if the chronometer readings were correct and whether the signal was a distress signal or a natural phenomenon.

"Commander, I have something." Lieutenant Samuel Jones reported. "The signal is definitely not natural. It is from one of our ships."

"Good work lieutenant, try raising them on the comm."

"Aye sir."

"Captain Valentine, report to the bridge." Jill called over the ships internal comm.

Robert was in his ready room, researching data on this system and what could be waiting when his first officer called for him.

"Commander, we are receiving an automated response, audio only." Lt. Jones said.

"What do we have?" Robert asked as he took his place in the captain's chair.

"Captain, we have confirmed the signal as being from a fleet ship, and we have received an automated audio response." Jill said as she turned over command.

"Let's hear what they have to say." Robert said. "If we have a fleet ship out there, I want to know what is going on."

An automated response began playing over the ships comm. "This is Captain Edward Smith of the U.S.S. Galileo to any ship within range. Our fleet entered a wormhole near the planet Earth, located approximately 4.3 light years from our current location. If you are --"

"Sir, that is all, the message is corrupted." Lt. Jones said.

"Send the following message," Robert said. "This is Captain Robert Valentine of the flag ship U.S.S. Jean-Pierre to any ship in range. Our ship's chronometer has indicated a two hundred year gap and we are working to determine if this is a malfunction or if the wormhole we entered displaced time and space in some way. If you are hearing this message, please respond."

"Message sent sir." Lt. Jones said.

"Captain, we should be arriving in orbit in less than one hour. Scans indicate orbital satellites and other technology." Jill said.

"Jones, you have the bridge, Commander Wright, join me in my ready room."

♦

"Jill, we have to consider the possibility that we are about to encounter an alien culture." Robert said.

"I agree. The problem we have right now is that a lot of our systems are still in transit mode. The crew is working to bring it all online as soon as possible. If I may suggest, perhaps we should hold our current location."

Door chime

"Enter." Robert said.

Ensign Madison Orr, a young ensign on her first assignment entered. "Sir, I am sorry for interrupting you, the sensors are now fully operational. We have completed a full scan. Long range sensors show that the satellites appear to be inactive."

"Good job ensign, scan the entire system for signs of active technology." Robert said; he and his first officer now joining everyone on the bridge. "Helm, all stop."

"Aye, answering all stop." The helmsman responded.

"Lieutenant Jones, scan all of this entire sector. I want to know if a speck of space dust moves."

"Aye Captain."

"Captain! Sensors are picking up a ship bearing two-four-seven mark three." Ensign Orr announced.

"Lay in a course. I want to know who we are dealing with."

"Aye sir, course laid in."

"Let's see who's out there." Robert said. "Engage."

The Jean-Pierre was on a new mission now. A mission to find her lost comrades. Captain Valentine waited in his ready room, a small office space just off the main bridge. Though the fleet was designed for deep space exploration, the ships were not very large. Each vessel was capable of supporting a crew regiment of up to one hundred and could carry an additional one hundred or so passengers. With the exception of the Jean-Pierre as it was the flag ship and offered a little more convenience for it's crew and passengers. Each ship was equipped with the latest in earth defense technology (E.D.T.), including a new shielding system and weaponry.

Robert Valentine was on his first mission and already facing a multitude of problems. A lost fleet. A planet whose satellites for some reason were non-functional. A different time. The list could go on. His crew was more than willing to help find answers as to what happened to his fleet. A first officer who was eager to serve, yet still new to her roles and learning. In fact, it was a learning process for them all, one that would surely lead to even more adventures in their lives and to new frontiers. The goal for now? Find the fleet. While the Jean-Pierre may have been equipped with the latest tech, they still needed to get all of that tech operational.

Chief Engineer, Commander Gordon Lafayette, worked trying to bring the experimental engines online. "Engineering to bridge, I think we are almost ready."

"Good work commander, keep me posted." Jill said.

"Sir, the signal is becoming stronger." Lt. Jones announced.

"Estimated time of arrival at our current rate?" Robert asked.

"At this rate sir," Jones said. "It will take approximately eight hours to reach the destination."

"Captain," Jill said. "If Commander Lafayette can get the new engines online we can cut that time in half. I suggest we hold our position, since we don't know what is waiting for us. We will want those engines in the event we need a way to reach safety."

"Agreed." Robert said. "Helm, all stop."

"Answering all stop sir."

◆

"Ensign, I need those engines now." Lafayette ordered as he and his engineering crew worked to bring the main engines online.

"Aye sir. System should be coming online now." Ensign Smith, said. A young science officer, eager to please.

"Alright everyone," Lafayette said. "Listen up. We are about to activate a very powerful system. This is a highly experimental and possibly dangerous process, based on early to mid 21st century ideas of an antimatter engine. This will be a mixture of matter and antimatter, creating a controlled reaction that should, in theory, allow us to bend space around us. Allowing for greater speeds."

"Commander," Smith said. "The system is online."

"Great job ensign. Prepare the chamber for matter-antimatter mix." Lafayette said. "If this is successful, we are about to witness the most powerful engineering feat of our time."

While an antimatter engine had been in the works prior to the chaotic events on earth over the past one hundred years, or at least as of the time of launching the fleet, the use of a matter-antimatter collision chamber to harness energy and convert that energy to allow for the bending or warping of time and space was all new. The mix had to be just right, the particles that were created had to be introduced in a certain way.

The engines were equipped with the latest in gamma radiation shielding to protect the crew and ship from the high radiation levels that would be produced. This was still experimental. All of this was based on the 21st century technology from the CERN program.

"Captain," Lafayette called over the comm. "We are ready."

♦

"Attention everyone," Captain Valentine began over the ship's comm. "We are about to embark on a new mission, this mission will undoubtedly take us to new levels in our growth as explorers and in our development as a species."

The ship began to hum as the engines were brought online. If it could be described, it felt like millions of wasps were inside the walls of the vessel, all buzzing around trying to find their way out. A sound of power like they have never felt before.

"Captain," Lafayette called over the comm. "The engines are online and ready."

"Perfect," Robert said. "I am going to give control over to engineering for this first run. I want full control in your hands."

"Aye sir, understood. I want to run a couple more tests before we attempt a warp jump."

"Understood, it is in your hands. Keep me posted."

Engineering would run more tests over the next hour, making sure that every aspect of the new engines were as safe as could be, considering that they were experimental. Robert knew he had to take the risk, he had a mission, to locate his missing fleet. Although they could make the trip using the ship's thrusters, it would take more time. Robert wanted to find his fleet, he needed to find them. He also knew they would need these new engines, just in case.

Chapter Seven
The True Mission
Earth 2105

"Frank, what is wrong?" Jean-Pierre asked. "What is going on with you?"

"I am unsure, but something is not right. I can feel a change in time. It is part of my --" He paused.

"Your what?"

"Programming."

Jean-Pierre stood looking at his grandson, trying to absorb what he had just heard.

"Programming?" He questioned. "Are you saying that you are some sort of machine?"

"No. Not entirely. I am human, however, I have a bio-chip that gives me abilities beyond that of a typical human."

"I think you owe me an explanation."

Frank informed his grandfather of his true mission. The fleet had made contact with a race of highly advanced beings. They had been monitoring earth for a long time, in fact, they visit earth quite frequently. When Frank left, to return to this time, the fleet was thriving and doing well, albeit missing some of the ships. His biotechnology allowed him to stay in contact with the future. However, the changes that were made have also changed his future and that of the fleet.

"So you're saying," Jean-Pierre began. "The future has changed and now the fleet is in more trouble?"

Frank thought carefully before answering.

"Honestly, I do not know. I do know this. I have a connection to the time-lines, thanks to the Centaurians, I can feel and know the events of time-lines from the past and certain parts of the future. At least to what would be my present time-line."

"What happened to the time-line?"

"Something changed. The fleet went through the wormhole at an earlier time. This caused a fluctuation in the fabric of space and time. The Jean-Pierre exited the wormhole two hundred years later. This appears to happen in both versions of the time-lines. However, there is a difference. Something changed."

"So, let me get this straight. You are some kind of cyborg?"

"No. I am human. With biotechnology."

"So, a cyborg."

Frank was growing irritated with this conversation.

"If you prefer, then yes, a cyborg."

"I remember a team of researchers who were experimenting with some kind of microchip that would create a super human. Is this something like that?"

"It is exactly that. Those researchers were experimenting with alien technology. Humans have been experimenting on *aliens* for over one hundred years, since the early twentieth century. In fact, many of those were the Centaurians."

"Many? You mean there are more?"

Frank laughed.

"There is so much you do not understand about the universe."

"Are you saying there are more?"

"Let's just say the Centaurians are the good guys."

"What is going on here?" Sara asked as she entered the room.

"Well," Jean-Pierre began. "For starters, our grandson is not who or what he appears. He is a cyborg!"

"Cyborg?"

This intrigued Sara and she wanted to hear more about this. She waited for an explanation.

"Let me explain, please. I am not a cyborg, not as you would perceive me to be. Although I do have biotechnology that allows me to do things other humans cannot, I am not a cyborg."

"You have an implant don't you?"

Sara was familiar with microchip technology the government had been experimenting with. However, she did not know that this technology was from extraterrestrials.

"Yes." Frank said. "Let me explain. When the fleet first arrived in the Alpha Centauri system, they were welcomed by a race of beings, called the Centaurians. At least that is what the fleet called them. An advanced civilization. They welcomed everyone with open arms, allowing them to live among them. When they learned of the chaos here on earth, they chose the one human with the DNA capable of handling their biotechnology. That one human was me."

"Wow." Sara whispered.

"So, again, you are a cyborg." Jean-Pierre said.

"No dear, he is not a cyborg. A cyborg would have mechanical and biological parts. He has a microchip that sends signals to his brain and nervous system. It also works with his muscular skeletal system, I would assume."

"That is correct." Frank said.

"So, no, he is not a cyborg. He is more defined as, well, as a super human."

"Frank," Jean-Pierre began. "It is time you told us everything."

"It will be a long story."

They all sat around the table as Frank told them the mission and what was at stake. He also told them what he was feeling, and how he was able to have such a connection with the time-lines. It was part of the technology from the Centaurians. This was a race that had been visiting earth for hundreds of years, as they monitored the development of the planet. Capable of a form of time travel, they had visited earth at many different times.

"If these beings are so powerful and concerned about us, why have they allowed all of this to happen?" Sara asked.

"It is not that simple. The Centaurians are a peaceful race, they must allow others to develop and grow as they choose.

They will not interfere in the free will of others as it is their birth right to grow and choose their own path with their inner life."

"Wait," Jean-Pierre said. "That sounds like some crazy anti war talk we see from all of these activist on earth."

"Exactly." Frank said. "Those movements were started when someone was introduced to a Centaurian who was embedded in the population to observe. When others saw their peaceful ways, they wanted to follow that lifestyle."

"So, you came back to change history? Doesn't that go against their beliefs?" Sara asked.

"Yes and no. They do not believe in changing history, at least not in major ways. They do, however, guide others in the path of good, but they must choose right from wrong. I came back to guide Faizan, sadly he chose a path of evil. In my human attempt to guide this project in the right path, I made mistakes. Mistakes that have cost more than it should have. Now I have to find a way to correct my mistakes."

"Centaurians sound like a Utopian race." Jean-Pierre said.

"They are a people of peace and tranquility. They have no war, no hate. They believe that all life is created to love."

"Wow," Sara said. "It sounds heavenly."

Over the past one hundred years, many people had forgotten the ways of their ancestors and had abandoned religion, however, there were still quite a few who held onto their faith. Sara was one of those few. Jean-Pierre on the other hand, was a man of pure science and did not believe in a higher power, or rather, he questioned the existence.

"So, the Centaurians have evolved into a peaceful race. I am sure it took them a very long time." Jean-Pierre said.

"No, like all of the universe, the Centaurian people were created in perfection. But given free will to live. They chose to live in peace, with the knowledge that all life is created equal and created to love. Sadly, not all of creation chooses to do so."

Sara sat quietly, looking at her King James bible on the shelf. She reached for it, causing it to fall onto the table. As it fell, it opened to a verse, it was Colossians 1:16...

For by him were all things created, that are in heaven, and that are in earth, visible and invisible, whether they be thrones, or dominions, or principalities, or powers: all things were created by him, and for him:

"Jean-Pierre! Look!" Sara shouted.

"That is just a coincidence."

"I would not be too sure about that." Frank said. "There are powers that you do not fully understand."

"Are you trying to say that some all powerful being is causing some book to fall open on a table?" Jean-Pierre asked.

"Let's just say that the creator of all things, large and small, is more than capable of opening a book to show you he is real. It is your choice to except this." Frank said. "I have learned a great deal from the Centaurian people about life and creation."

"Okay, let's cut to the chase. You said something was wrong. So what is going on?"

"What do you mean?" Sara asked.

"Earlier, Frank here kept saying something was wrong."

"It is difficult to explain. The biotechnology that I have allows me to sense certain aspects of space and time. When the changes took place, the fleet left one year early. At first, there should have been no real issue. However, something happened, something was different."

"Wait," Jean-Pierre said. "There was a last minute change in the crew manifest for one of the ships."

"Explain." Frank said.

"Just before the launch date, the captain of the Galileo was replaced. He had been arrested by the New United Nations on charges of conspiracy to overthrow the One World Government. He was replaced by a new captain and senior crew."

"That is it. That is the changes I feel. He was not supposed to be replaced. I can sense a major change in the time-line, one that places the entire mission in danger. I must fix this."

"How can you fix it?" Sara asked.

"He is a traitor! He is just looking for an excuse to get out of here and turn us over to Faizan."

Jean-Pierre was agitated and now convinced that Frank had planned this all along.

"No, I can assure you I am not. This is truly upsetting to me. My family is in danger. I can no longer sense the Centaurians. I must find a way to repair this mistake."

"If you are not a traitor, then you won't mind me tagging along to make sure you don't mess up again, will you?"

"I cannot risk your life. Too many have perished, and I must correct this. It is my fault."

"Frank," Sara began. "What can you do?"

"I must return to my time-line, at a point prior to me leaving. At that point, I will find a way to stop my returning here. At least at this time. Instead, I will return a few days prior. This should allow me to reset the time-lines and prevent the captain from being arrested. There is just one issue --"

Chapter Eight
The Lost Fleet

Alpha Centauri System, 2305

"Robert," Jill said as the two discussed the current situations in his ready room. "I know you want to find the others, but I think we should be prepared for anything. We are not sure what we will find."

"We will find them. We have to. There is so much at stake here, and those satellites, I can't get them off my mind."

"I know, it is strange. I think we should investigate more."

"Agreed."

The two made their way onto the bridge, Robert had decided more information was needed in regards to this system and those satellites.

"Ensign Orr, I want more scans on those satellites. We need to know what happened here."

"Aye captain."

"Engineering, status?" Commander Wright inquired.

"Lafayette here, it is going to be a while, the best I can give you right now are the thrusters."

"Understood. Keep working on those new engines."

"Aye commander, give me another hour at least."

"Captain, this can't be right."

"What is it ensign?

"The satellites sir, they --"

"They are what?" Jill asked.

"They appear to be man made, of earth based materials."

"Helm, set course to that planet and engage full thrusters. I want to know what is going on here."

"Aye captain."

"Captain," Ensign Orr began. "Sensors indicate these satellites have been inactive for at least one hundred years."

Robert looked at Jill, she knew what he was thinking. If the rest of the fleet had arrived earlier, by some chance. It was possible they had established a colony. Now, they needed to know what happened to that colony.

"Robert," Jill said softly. "You don't think it could be them, do you?"

"I am not sure Jill, but there are satellites here that appear to be made by humans. I want to know what happened."

"Sir, I am detecting a faint signal, coming from one of the moons." Orr reported. "It appears to be coming from beneath the surface."

"A moon base?" Jill questioned, looking towards the captain.

"But is it ours?" Robert responded.

The Jean-Pierre arrived in orbit around the moon where the signal originated. The answer to many questions was awaiting below. Now, a new question: what would they find?

"Jill, you have the ship. I am heading this mission."

"No Robert, your place is here. I must insist."

"I have to know what is down there."

"You will, but your safety is priority to this mission. I will head the team and report back. I am not arguing this, it is my job to make sure the captain remains safe, as your first officer."

"Very well."

"Lieutenant Commander Ellis, report to the shuttle bay. Orr you are with me."

Jill, Orr and now Security Chief Mark Ellis boarded the shuttle craft Endurance and prepared for departure. This would be a blind mission, meaning that the crew was heading into a situation with little to no knowledge of what was waiting for them. It would be dangerous.

"Shuttle craft Endurance is ready for departure." Jill said over the comm. "Jones, maintain an open comm with us at all times."

"Aye commander."

"Godspeed my friend." Robert said.

"Endurance away, sir." Jones announced.

Good luck my friend. Find our fleet and bring them home.

Robert stood, watching the monitor as the shuttle craft made her final approach to this alien world. Hoping for the best, but expecting the worst. The satellites indicated at least a century had passed. The chances were slim, but not impossible. If, by chance, they had entered stasis once again, they could theoretically survive.

"Endurance to Jean-Pierre, we have found something. I'm taking us in for a closer look."

"Be careful Jill." Robert said.

"It appears to be an entrance to an underground facility of some type. There seems to be writing on the entrance. Wait, what is this?"

"What is it Jill? What do you see?"

"The writing is not from our fleet. There are symbols on the entrance that I do not recognize. Wait, something is hap --"

The signal was cut, they lost communication.

"Jones, get them back!" Robert commanded.

"I am trying sir." Jones answered. "Sir, look! There seems to be some type of beam coming from the entrance, it's pulling them inside."

"Do we have weapons online?" Robert asked.

"No sir, we are still waiting on systems to fully reboot. They will not be ready for at least one hour."

"I need those weapons now!"

"Aye sir, I will do my best." Lafayette replied.

We're coming Jill, hold on my friend. Hold on.

"Helm, can we take the ship in any closer?"

"No sir, not without risking a crash."

Robert paced in front of the monitor, watching as his first officer and crew members were being pulled into an unknown facility. He was feeling angry and frustrated.

I should not have sent them on this mission.

◆

"Ensign, I need more power to the engines! We need to break free from this beam!" Jill commanded.

"I am trying commander! We can't break free!"

"Commander, weapons are offline." Ellis reported.

"Open a channel!" Jill said.

"Channel open." Orr responded.

"This is Commander Jillian Wright of the U.S.S. Jean-Pierre, we are here on a peaceful mission."

"Message sent commander."

"Do we have contact with the Jean-Pierre yet?"

"No sir, we have lost all communication with the ship, we only have short range sensors and comm."

Robert my friend, I hope you find a way to save us.

"Commander, the beam has stopped pulling us in. But it still has us locked." Ellis reported.

"Send the message again."

"Aye commander, message sent." Orr said. "I am detecting something from within the facility. A signal is coming in, but I am not sure what it is, it is in a language I have never heard."

"Try to get a fix on it's origin."

"The signal is changing. It is now coming in English. But it is broken."

"Broken?" Jill asked.

"Yes, it is coming across in a broken and distorted message."

"Put it on audio."

A broken message began playing over the shuttle's audio.

"Ship, destruction, must not allow. Ship, destruction, must not allow."

"Commander, it is just repeating the same message."

◆

"Captain, I am detecting a signal coming from the facility, a message is being sent to the shuttle." Jones said.

"Can you get a fix on it?"

"No sir."

"I want to know what or who we are dealing with here!"

Hold on my friend, hold on. We are going to save you and your team.

"Captain, the message is as follows 'Ship, destruction, must not allow,' sir, it just repeats." Jones turned to his captain, waiting for the next order.

"Do we have communication with the shuttle yet?"

"No captain, I am still trying to reestablish a link."

"Captain Valentine," Lafayette said as he entered the bridge. "I have good news and bad news. The good news is, we have the new engines ready to go. The bad news is, the top *speed* would be equivalent to only two times that of light speed. Of course as you know, we won't be actually traveling at that speed, rather we are bending or warping space around us in a bubble of sorts."

"I am well aware of how the engines work commander. Right now I have a shuttle crew in trouble and no weapons."

"Aye, that is the other thing I want to talk about. The weapons system has been disabled."

"Disabled?! By whom?"

"That is the odd one captain, it appears a jamming signal from the moon, it was undetectable, but has disabled our defenses."

"I want answers! Who are we dealing with?"

Robert Valentine was an easy going captain, however, when it came to his crew and friends, he could be very strong willed. He wanted answers, but answers were not available at this time. It was not just his crew, it was his friends that were seemingly under attack. He swore under his breath as he watched helplessly.

♦

"Commander, a new message is coming across, this time it is a little more clear. Audio only." Orr said.

"On speakers."

"Attention humans. Your previous attack on our home world caused much damage. We are a race of peace keepers, we were created to be a race of peace. We are not attacking you, but we will not allow you to bring harm to our base. We would like to talk."

"Commander, I have weapons back! I can take them out with one shot!" Ellis exclaimed.

"No! Hold your position. We will see what they have to say. Open a channel."

"Channel open." Orr said.

"This is Commander Jillian Wright of the U.S.S. Jean-Pierre, we are here on a peaceful mission. We did not attack your home world, we just arrived in this system."

Silence filled the air as they waited for a response. It was as if time had frozen, as they anticipated their first contact response. Jill, now feeling bad that Robert was not with them to witness this in person, was considering her next message.

"This is Commander Jillian Wright of the U.S.S. Jean-Pierre, we are here on a peaceful mission. Our captain is Robert Valentine, he is on-board the Jean-Pierre, we are only here for a search and rescue mission. Please, allow us to return to the ship and we will arrange to talk, perhaps face to face."

"Message sent." Orr said.

"Maintain an open channel." Jill said, as she waited the reply.

"Commander, the beam has released." Ellis reported.

"Take us out of here, slowly." Jill commanded. "Thank you for trusting us. We will return to the ship. Please stand by for contact information with our captain."

♦

"Captain, the shuttle is returning. The comm is still down or being jammed." Jones reported.

"Get them back and let's find out what is going on. Have there been any other messages?

"Aye sir, I was just able to access the last message sent to the shuttle, it reads as follows: 'Attention humans. Your previous attack on our home world caused much damage. We are a race of peace keepers, we were created to be a race of peace. We are not attacking you, but we will not allow you to bring harm to our base. We would like to talk.' That was last message they received sir."

The shuttle craft Endurance docked and Jill made her way to meet with Robert in his ready room. They were about to make first contact with an alien race. Things had to be ready and they had lots of questions about the missing fleet.

"Robert," Jill began as she entered the ready room. "We have a chance to make a difference, but something seemed off. They said something about an attack, as if we had attacked them."

"Yes, we intercepted the message. It is strange. Also, I have learned something about the Galileo. It appears that the message we heard, presumably from Captain Smith, was false. According to pre-launch records, Smith was replaced before the mission began. In fact, his entire bridge crew was replaced at the last minute."

"That sounds odd. Why would they do that at the last minute?"

"I am not sure," Robert replied. "I am now wondering if it has anything to do with our alien friends down there."

"The message said something about a previous attack. The fact that we were captured by some type of confinement beam, and those disabled satellites that appear to be of human design, it all fits together." Jill said.

Door chimes

"Enter." Robert said.

"Sir, we are receiving a transmission." Jones said as he entered the ready room. "They are asking for a meeting and request the meeting be held on the Jean-Pierre."

"Make the arrangements. Commander Wright and I will meet them at the docking port."

"Sir, they have requested permission to transport."

"Transport?"

"Aye, we questioned their request. Apparently they have the ability to teleport or something."

"Things are starting to make more sense. Back on earth, there had been research with technology to allow for teleportation. It appears our friends may have been to earth in the past, and our scientist have been reverse engineering technology. Have them to transport at their discretion."

"Aye sir."

Robert and Jill discussed options among themselves before returning to the bridge. They were about to make first, official contact with an advanced alien race, who apparently have been to earth in the past. Would there be issues in regards to past events by humans? Would there be consequences for the apparent actions of the fleet against their home world?

◆

"They are ready to transport sir." Lt. Commander Ellis said.

"Okay everyone, let's treat this as a high level diplomatic event, I want them to feel welcome and safe. Weapons will remain checked at all times, unless a security threat arrives. We do not know what they will look like, so I expect the utmost respect in those regards." Robert said.

"Aye sir!" The bridge crew responded in unison.

"Signal them that we are ready."

"Aye sir." Jones responded.

The crew watched as a beam of light appeared before them on the main bridge. Particles could be seen in the light, merging and forming into solid matter. It was like something out of an old movie from the 20th century. The light faded and standing before the crew were four individuals. Humanoid beings, they had a tall, slender build, with long arms fingers. Their skin was pale with a gray-tone and large eyes. Almost fitting the description of the Grays described in the 20th and 21st centuries. Clothed in robes, that shimmered in the light.

"Welcome aboard the U.S.S. Jean-Pierre, I am Captain Robert Valentine, this is my first officer, Commander Jillian Wright."

"We are the Council of Centaur. I believe you know our world as Proxima b." The taller of the four aliens said.

"May I ask your name?" Robert asked.

"In your language, I would be called Gizelle Oorurah, Minister for the Council of Centaur. You may call me Gizelle or Minister, if you choose."

"Welcome aboard Minister. We are pleased to meet you. Please forgive me if we seem shocked. It's just, your appearance seems to fit the description of beings that visited our planet hundreds of years ago."

"Indeed," Minister Gizelle said. "We have visited many worlds, including Earth."

"You know who we all are, who are your friends?" Robert asked as he motioned for everyone to take a seat.

"This is my council, you may address me at all times. They are here as observers only."

"Okay," Robert said, rather puzzled at his response. "Why did you attack our shuttle?"

"Attack? We did not attack, only disabled. We are a peaceful species. We do not condone violence of any form. Your planet has been plagued by violence for millennia, dating back to the creation of your known world."

"Yes, we have had our share of wars and violent moments, it is definitely not something we are proud of." Jill said.

"We have been monitoring your progress, in hopes that one day, you would change your ways, to be what you were created to be. Sadly, that has not happened."

"Their species has come a long way minister." One of the council members stated.

"Silence." Minister Gizelle said in a calm but firm voice. "You are here to observe, not speak."

"I am not sure I understand what you are saying." Robert said.

"Since the dawn of man, your species was given the freedom to choose right from wrong, good from evil. Sadly, many of you chose the latter. This was not the will of the Creator, but he chose to allow you that freedom."

"You speak of the creator, are you referring to a god? I mean, I know our planet has a history of worshiping gods."

"Robert, I believe he is referring to God, in the biblical sense. I have always believed that the bible was true, even though so many have left the faith." Jill said.

"Yes," Minister Gizelle said. "In your history, your people knew the Creator as God. He is known by many names and he is the creator of everything."

"Okay, this is all well and good, but what does all of that have to do with any of this or my missing fleet?" Robert asked.

"Around two hundred years ago, earth time, a ship arrived in our system. Our people welcomed these visitors from earth, hoping that your species had grown and moved beyond the evil that has plagued your world. Sadly, this was not the case. When they found that we were not a violent people, they attacked us. We had no choice but to surrender. Thousands of our people died. Others became slaves. Over the years, many of us escaped and spread out in this system, building colonies. The council chose to build a base here, to monitor our home world."

Robert sat quiet, not sure how he should respond. He knew that the ship he was referencing had to be the Galileo. But, where were the others? If the Galileo arrived in the same time period as when we left, then that means the wormhole was a success in being a viable means of inter-galactic travel to other worlds. The question remains though, why did the Jean-Pierre arrive when they did and where were the others?

"I understand your not being a violent people, but can you not defend yourselves?" Lieutenant Commander Ellis asked.

"We have never needed planetary defenses, nor have we needed weapons. Therefore, that leaves us with no way to defend ourselves."

"Forgive me Minister," Robert said. "I understand your people have visited our planet in the past, and I presume that is why you can speak our language so well. However, in your inter-galactic travels, you never thought that a time would arise that you would need to defend yourselves?"

Minister Gizelle spoke with his council briefly in their home language. Leaving the crew to question what they were saying. Were they offended? Was there more to them that was being seen? Robert was sure there had to be more.

"Our mission was to observe only, however, you should be warned --"

"Warned?" Ellis interrupted the council minister.

"Yes. Understand, we are not the only race in the creation. Some chose to live in peace, as was intended. However, just as your world has been plagued by violence, others have been as well and many of them chose to live that life and to conquer."

"Forgive me," Jill said. "You speak of our history, the arrival of the missing ship and everything as if you were around. I hope this does not offend, but just how old are you?"

"Jill!" Robert retorted to his first officer.

"No worries captain. Yes commander, we have a long history. We live for hundreds of years, until the Creator chooses to take us to a higher level of existence to live with him in his realm."

"I find this all interesting, but that doesn't answer my questions as to what happened, what does this have to do with my fleet?" Robert was growing impatient.

"You mention a fleet. Only two ships have emerged from your wormhole. The one that arrived and decimated our world and yours. If there are other ships, they could have emerged at a different time or, sadly, they could have been destroyed."

"There are a number of satellites around your home world, they appear to be man-made, of earth design. Can you tell us what happened to them?" Ellis asked.

"After the ship emerged and our people were defeated, they used their technology to establish a base, in hopes to one day, communicate with earth. They could not understand our language, and to protect the innocent lives on your world and others, we chose to maintain our identity. Unable to learn our technology and language, they began to die off. The world was not suitable to sustain human life. Eventually the technology wasted away."

"What happened to your people?" Robert asked.

"We are spread throughout this system and the galaxy."

"This is ridiculous!" Ellis shouted. "Lies, it's all lies!"

"Ellis! That will be enough! You're relieved of duty until further notice." Jill ordered. "Report to your quarters and remain there until I call for you."

"Minister Gizelle, I apologize for my officer's actions. It will not happen again." Robert said.

"That is quite alright captain. He is visibly upset."

"As an officer, he should be in control of his emotions and be able to contain them." Jill said.

"I think that is the ultimate goal for all those who choose peace in this vast universe." Minister Gizelle said.

"If we may get back to the missing fleet." Robert said. "You stated that the one ship appeared around two hundred years ago, which is when we left earth. However, the others have not appeared. We arrived just recently. So, what happened?"

"A wormhole, depending on the conditions, can be a fast form of travel to reach far destinations at what would seem to be, faster than light travel. However, if the conditions are off, even a little, it can cause a ripple in the fabric of space and time."

"What you are saying then," Jill said. "The other ships could be arriving at a later date than we did?"

"Yes, that is possible."

"I have one more question, before we go any further." Robert said, curious as to how a species could live so long and have access to space travel with no visible means of ships. "You have, or your people have visited earth in the past, so how did you get there?"

"We have been traveling the universe for thousands of your years. Our scientists developed what you would call 'warp travel' over one thousand earth years ago. Before that, we had access to artificial wormhole technology. Similar to what you used to get here."

"Yes, my father found a way to harness particles, converting them to energy that resulted in the wormhole." Robert said.

"The method we detected was very familiar. But we have not used wormhole travel in millennia."

"Are you saying my father is not intelligent enough to discover this method?"

"Not at all, the only problem is, the one element needed does not exist on earth. It is only found on our home world."

"That would mean, my father had access to alien technology."

"Yes and no. The element, known as Element X on our world would not remain stable on your planet for a long period of time. Meaning that someone had to carry it to earth."

"How could an alien species be on earth during these times without being caught? Our current government, or at least the one we left behind, would take them to experiment on with no questions." Jill said.

"Yes, if they knew who was there. We have the ability to alter our appearance to appear human. But I am not sure that is what happened here."

Chapter Nine
A Broken Time-Line
Earth, 2105

"Frank, if you are still here, then something is still active in the future that has not changed." Sara said.

"This is true. It would appear my parents survive, furthermore, the scientists who gave me the implant and ability to travel in time, also survive."

"You have been saying that something has changed. Are you sure it was something regarding your visit to this time-line? I mean, it is apparent that nothing major changed, because you are still here." Jean-Pierre said.

"No, something is different, as I said, I have a connection with the time-lines and there has been a major shift in events that led to loss of life."

The implant not only allowed Frank to travel through time, he also had a type of ESP, or Extrasensory Perception that allowed him to see things, or rather sense things. Although there has been experiments with ESP and Psychic abilities among humans, this was indeed a huge leap in that field, to tap into the abilities and amplify them.

"Frank, do you have ESP?" Sara asked.

"Where I am from, humans are born with great abilities. The conditions that are presented to humans create longer life spans, an increase in muscular skeletal development, higher brain function and more. We are stronger, smarter and more capable than our ancestors."

"All of this because of the implant, right?" Jean-Pierre asked.

"No, this is our natural development. The implant only allows me to tap into these abilities and focus them more. For example, the frontal lobe, the part of the brain that controls high-

-level cognitive skills and primary motor functions, is more advanced in us. This allows us to access those, for a lack of better terms, primitive abilities of ESP and other psychic tendencies. Add the implant and now it allows me *see* things across a great distance including time."

"Wait, in the twentieth century, the government was said to have experimented with a program called *project stargate* which was reported to use a person with psychic abilities to remote view locations far away." Sara said.

"Yes, that is exactly what this is. The only difference? We are much better."

"Wow, that sounds so conceded." Jean-Pierre said.

"Not at all, that is not what I meant it to be. It is, fact. It has nothing to do with feeling that we are better, it is the truth. Not that I am trying to say you or anyone else do not matter. It is in our DNA and the environmental conditions allow us to develop to this level."

"Okay, so aside from the cognitive and physical abilities, you were given technology by the Centaurians." Sara said. "My question is why?"

"Honestly, I do not remember. Something has happened and it is affecting my abilities to sense the time-lines. I know that there was a battle, no, not a battle. It was an attack that took place. I remember being told that my parents stopped the attack. But after that, I am losing that connection. I must return now. Only the Centaurian people can find the answers."

Frank knew something was wrong and the longer he waited, the more he was losing of his connection to the time-lines. The question remains; what happened? He remembers an attack, that was apparently stopped by Robert Valentine and his crew, but something was off with this now. Something changed and he knew that his actions were the cause of this change. Would it make a difference? Would it be the end to humanity as they knew it? He had to find a way to fix this and he knew the answer was in the future, if there was a future he could return to.

"If there is something wrong with the future as you know or knew it, is it safe for you to return?" Jean-Pierre asked.

"He has no choice my love, he must return."

"She is right, I must return."

"What do we need for you to activate the wormhole back to your time-line?" Jean-Pierre asked.

"It is part of my implant, I have the ability to open portals. I must be in an open area, outside."

"Then let's get you outside."

"Frank, be careful," Sara said. "If the time-lines are in fact changed, you could be returning to an entirely different scenario."

"Sara is right. What if you return and everything is gone?"

"It may be changed, but I do not think it has been destroyed. If that were the case, I do not think I would still be here. I can also sense my mentor; Gizelle, Council Minister of Centaur."

"You have a connection to the aliens?" Jean-Pierre asked.

"Not in a way of communication, however I can sense a part of their life, their spirits. You could call it a spiritual connection."

"That's amazing." Sara said.

"Yeah, I think it is called technology." Jean-Pierre scoffed. He was not a religious man by any means, and he found the topic of spirits and creation to be fantasy. He was a man of science. Although, science has proven many times to be more than what one sees.

"I understand your skepticism, however, don't underestimate what you can't see. Remember, the particles discovered in your experiments were once unseen, in fact, they were created. If we humans can create new particles by colliding others together, then why can't there be a being with even higher intelligence who created life as we know it. In fact, I remember something from my earth history class, of a scientist in the early 21st century who theorized that the universe, as we know it, could have been created in a laboratory in some alternate or parallel universe."

"Well, there are scientist out there who believe that, but I am a realist, I want to see facts. That is why I work so hard to find answers. However, as a scientist, I must also look at all things with an open mind."

"Very good." Frank said. "Now, I must go. It is time for me to return. It was great to meet my grandparents in person. My father has told me so much about you. I pray you remain safe and that my journey will repair the changes that took place."

"Please, be careful." Sara said, as she gave Frank a gentle kiss on the cheek.

"Yes, be careful and I hope you find the answers to fix all of this." Jean-Pierre added.

Frank made his way to a clearing where he could activate the wormhole. He would need a large opening for the event horizon to form. Once opened, he would be able to guide his path back to the Centaur home world. Tapping into his implant, Frank opened a wormhole to the Alpha Centauri system.

As the event horizon formed, Jean-Pierre and Sara watched in amazement at the power their grandson possessed. Frank stood, as if he were trying to decide his next step.

"Something is wrong." Sara said.

The wormhole began to close.

"What is he doing?" Jean-Pierre asked.

Frank walked back toward his grandparents, a look of despair upon his face.

"Frank?" Sara questioned as he approached their side.

"They -- they are not there." He said, in a monotone voice.

"What do you mean?" Jean-Pierre asked.

"The home world is vacant of all life."

"But you said you could sense your mentor." Sara said.

"Yes, and I still can. But they are not on the home world. I need a moment to myself. I must pray."

"Seriously?" Jean-Pierre asked. "We are dealing with this and he wants to pray!"

"Come, let him pray."

The Valentines went back to the lab while Frank sat quietly, praying and meditating. She could sense that her grandson had a spiritual connection and she knew he had to do this.

"This is all ridiculous." Jean-Pierre said. "Praying isn't going to help. We need him to tap into his implant and get back to his time-line and fix this."

"Jean-Pierre, you need to understand, science and God can coexist together. They work hand in hand. He created it all."

"Sara, you know how I feel about religion. I mean, I do not know if there is some higher power at work in the universe. As far as I am concerned, it could be an advanced alien species."

"One day, my love, you will understand and you will know the truth."

Sara was optimistic to say the least. She believed there was good in everyone, if they would just listen to their heart. She knew her husband was a caring man, and that meant there was a chance he would change his views. After all, she was praying for him daily.

◆

Frank spent at least two hours meditating and praying, seeking answers. The Centaurian people were very close to the Creator, and had guided him in his own spiritual path. After his time of prayer he returned to the lab with the answers they all were waiting to hear.

"I have the answers I needed." Frank said.

"What did you learn?" Sara asked.

"Probably how to sleep while we wait." Jean-Pierre retorted sarcastically.

"I understand your skepticism, however, my prayers have led me to the answers we are seeking. My mentor is alive. I did detect him among the time-lines, it appears that the Jean-Pierre made contact, but at a nearby moon instead. I will attempt the jump again, but I feel we need to wait for a short while."

"Wait?" Jean-Pierre asked.

"Yes. We need to give the time-lines a chance to *reset*."

"I think I understand," Sara said as she poured them all a glass of tea. "Since the changes have affected different aspects of the time-lines, the changes are still taking place across time."

"Yes, that is the best way to explain it. Decisions are being made right now in my parent's time of arrival that will ultimately affect how the future plays out."

"What if you return to their time and tell them what happened, maybe something can be done." Jean-Pierre said.

"No," Sara said. "That could definitely cause a paradox."

"Okay, this time travel is really getting on my nerves. Sara, you and Frank figure this out, I am going for a walk."

This is getting ridiculous, I need some fresh air before I go crazy in my old age.

With Jean-Pierre out for walk, this left Sara and Frank to find answers to their multiple time-line dilemma. If Frank returns too soon and warns his parents of the events to come, he could cause an irreversible paradox. If he returns to his time before the changes take place, he could arrive to a war zone or worse. This was going to require a lot of research to determine the best options. Or, perhaps a lot of prayer.

Chapter Ten
A New Time-Line Begins
A Nearby Moon of Proxima b, 2305

Minister Gizelle talked with the council, trying to decide the next step in this disaster of a first contact mission. The attack on their home world was not what this mission needed, but sadly it had already taken place. It was up to Captain Valentine and his crew to find a way to move things forward for a truly peaceful relationship.

"Captain Valentine." Minister Gizelle said. "As I have stated, we are a peaceful people. We are also a forgiving people. We cannot hold your crew responsible for the actions of the others who arrived before you."

"I appreciate the opportunity to develop a mutual friendship with your people."

"We will work with you and your crew to help locate the missing ships. However, you must understand that your trust must be earned."

"We understand."

"If you will allow us to help, we will return to our temporary home. From there, we can access the time-lines to determine the approximate time and location of your missing ships. You are welcome to join us."

"Wow. You can do that?"

"It is one of our abilities that allows us to travel the universe and visit other worlds at different times."

"You're time travelers?" Jill asked. She had been sitting quiet until now.

"If you prefer. Yes. We are able to manipulate time and space, to an extent."

"My question is," Robert said. "If you have this ability, then how were you attacked by someone of our status?"

"As I have stated, we are a peaceful people, we do not condone nor do we use violence."

"But you attacked our shuttle." Security Chief Ellis stated as he stood to his feet in protest of this statement.

"At ease Lieutenant Commander." Jill ordered. She had allowed him to return to duty. "That is a good question though."

"We did not attack your shuttle, rather we immobilized you and disengaged your weapons. After the attack, we immediately began to develop technology to protect our people in a non-violent manner."

"Okay," Robert began. "Why is such an advanced species not already protected?"

"While there are numerous worlds in the universe, Earth is our nearest contact. Your world has been under observation for a long time. Until now, no other species has reached our home world. In fact, most of the universe finds this part of the galaxy to be of no value."

"Why are the Centaurians interested in us?" Robert asked.

"Before the dawn of man, as you know it, our people was visiting your planet. We walked among, what your bible calls, the Angels as they cared for the creatures of that time."

"Wait," Jill said. "Angels?"

"Yes. They cared for the creatures, in your language, known as dinosaurs. A great war took place within their plain of existence, their universe if you so wish to refer. There was a rise against the Creator, to overthrow him and this band of traitors was cast out into this dimension, this universe, to earth. Earth was then struck by a catastrophic event. This brought on the extinction of many species. The creator then made the earth new, with a new creation of life. Mankind. He was pleased with this creation."

"So, you are talking about the genesis events, Adam and Eve and so forth." Robert interjected.

"Yes. In fact, this creation was intended to live close to the Creator, on a higher level than even our people. They were given the same freedom to choose as we were. Sadly, they chose to disobey the Creator, creating a curse on mankind."

"The original sin," Jill said. "When Eve partook of the forbidden fruit. That was what is referred to as the fall of man. The original sin."

"This is all well and good and a great story," Robert said. "But you are telling me that some being in an alternate universe wiped out the dinosaurs, created man, aliens and all that we see, yet so much evil exist in the world. If he is so powerful, then why does he allow it?"

"The Creator is an all powerful being who exists on a much higher plain, in fact, he has created all that you see and are aware of. He is also a caring creator. However, he will not allow pure evil to overtake. Those who betrayed him were cast out and those who choose to follow that path will also be cast away."

"It sounds like you are describing Satan and being cast into the lake of fire." Jill said.

Minister Gizelle thought for a moment before responding. He knew there was so much he could teach, but he also knew that mankind must choose the path on their own.

"As you understand it, yes."

"Okay," Robert said. "This is all well and good. It's a great story, but I am a man of science. This all seems so fictional."

"You say you are a man of science. I believe it is your own science that has theorized the existence of multiple universes and alternate dimensions. Also, your science has levels of civilization theories, a scale, that has theorized a civilization level with the ability to *create* universes."

Robert was silent. He had no response to this, as the minister was correct. In quantum theories, there was talk of alternate or parallel universes and dimensions.

What if, God does exist? He thought.

"Captain," Gizelle said. "We must return now, in order to start. You are welcome to join us."

Startled from his thoughts, Robert replied. "Oh, sure, I will prepare my crew. My first officer and I will join you shortly."

♦

Robert and Jill joined the Centaurian Council in the shuttle bay where they would return to the moon together. Gizelle assured them everything was safe.

"Shuttle craft Endurance to Jean-Pierre, ready for departure. All systems operational." Jill reported to the flight deck chief.

The Endurance departed and they were on their way to a new world, or in this case, moon. Jill piloted the shuttle while Robert talked with the minister to learn more of their history with earth.

He was still uncertain of this new history he was hearing. He grew up in a home where his father was a devout man of science, yet his mother was a Christian. There were quite a few times that an argument would take place when his mother would talk about the bible and God, but she stood firm on her beliefs and did her best to instill those beliefs into Robert.

"We are arriving at the docking bay." Jill said as she turned the shuttles controls over to the computer for auto docking.

"Excellent," Robert said. "Now maybe we can find answers as to what happened to my fleet.

"Do not despair my friends, I am sure we will." Gizelle said.

The shuttle docked and they all made their way to the base command center. Gizelle instructed his council members to contact the other Centaurian people. The plan was to return to the home world and reestablish their colony.

"Minister Gizelle," Robert said. "I have been thinking about our conversation. You talk about how your people have visited our planet in past, including that story of our creation.

But, I was curious -- If there is a God or Creator, why haven't we seen him?"

"That seems to be the age old question with your people. Your bible speaks of *faith*, you even rely on this same faith when you create something new trusting that it will work."

Robert interrupted. "But those things I can see."

"That is true, however, you can *see* the Creator all around you, in yourselves, in stars. He is all around in his creations. Just as humans see themselves in the things that they create, our Creator is in all that he has created."

"Okay, so have you met him personally? I mean, you *are* able to manipulate time and space."

The minister laughed as he answered. "We have all met him, in one way or another captain. It all depends on your perspective of the meaning. Your people are still living in a three dimensional view of the universe."

"God exists on an entirely different dimensional level," Jill said as she joined them. "We will only be able to experience that level of existence after our spirits leave these bodies."

"Yeah, I get the whole soul aspect, and I do not deny that even science has suggested that there is the possibility of a soul. But, I am still unsure of what that means. Is it an evolutionary state of our lives?" Robert said.

"I suppose," Gizelle said as he entered more information into a computer console that was more advanced than Robert or Jill had ever seen. "You could view it as an evolutionary process, but it is more of a transitional process to a new level."

"As I was saying," Robert continued, "your people can manipulate time and space. So, have you been to other dimensions?"

"No. We have not achieved that power, nor do we choose to. We understand that the Creator created many things, if we were to attempt to create an inter-dimensional portal to His realm, we would then be attempting to achieve his level of existence. We understand that this comes when we transition, so there is no need to use technology to achieve what the Creator has already made possible when it is time to join him in his realm."

An alarm began to sound.

"What is going on?" Jill asked.

"It appears your ship is attacking us." Gizelle said.

"Valentine to Ellis, what are you doing?!"

No response.

"Minister Gizelle, can you jam those weapons?" Jill asked.

"I am doing so now."

"Ellis! Respond!" Robert ordered over the comm.

A voice came over the comm, it was the security chief who had been left in charge and now betrayed his captain.

"Captain Valentine, I have taken control of this vessel and we *will* destroy this moon. All hail Faizan!"

The comm went silent.

"Faizan?" Robert and Jill questioned simultaneously.

"Minister Gizelle, can you get us on my ship?"

"I am sorry captain, it appears there attack has damaged our systems. The council is working on it now."

"Ellis! Why are you doing this? Stand down now and I will go easy on you." Robert said.

"Hello former captain. As you can see, I am in control of things now. Your friends may have jammed my weapons, but they have lost control of all other technology that can stop us. We will be returning to the wormhole to take vital information back to our supreme commander, Prime Minister Faizan."

"Ellis, you cannot do this." Jill said as she tried to reason with him. "Please, you must stop this. Faizan is a mad man who is out to rule the world and to murder innocent people."

Gizelle and his council continued to work on repairs, they knew if they could get the systems back online, there was a way to stop him without harming anyone.

"Minister Gizelle, we really need that beam you used on our shuttle!" Jill shouted across the room.

"It is online now. Activating the confinement beam now."

The Jean-Pierre was now confined by the Centaurians. But they still needed to gain access to the ship. Gizelle was about to introduce more of their technology to the captain.

"Captain Valentine, if I may suggest, we have other means to gain access besides your shuttle craft."

"Then let's get going!"

"As you have witnessed, we have the ability to transport matter through space, for short distances. It is a new technology, one we have only used once to visit your ship and to transport supplies to the moon base."

"Could you transport me to my ship?"

"It would be a risk. As your bodies are different than ours."

"I'll go Robert."

"No Jill, I cannot risk your life for my mistakes. I should have questioned the crew when we discovered what happened with the other crew."

"There is another way," Gizelle said. "We could transport your Mr. Ellis here. However, please understand, it is a risk. Normally we would not take such risks with lives, but in this case, I feel it is an acceptable risk."

"Do it." Robert ordered. "I mean, I understand and we will not hold you responsible for anything that may go wrong."

Gizelle approached a computer terminal on the far side of the room, after scanning the ship's interior he located Ellis. With a few commands, a particle beam appeared and a body began to materialize in front of them. Ellis was now there with them, unharmed but stunned.

"How did I get here?" Ellis asked as he looked around.

"You underestimated our friends," Robert said. "Now, I want to know how many more traitors are on my ship."

"Traitor?" Ellis laughed. "If anyone is a traitor, it is you and your family. However, to answer your question, I acted alone. Thanks to Prime Minister Faizan, I was equipped with a few high-tech tools before we left earth. Oh, I suppose we owe a little thanks to your friends, after all, it was there technology that we reversed engineered over the years."

"This is wrong." Gizelle said. "This is all wrong."

"What is it Minister?" Jill asked.

"This. This is all wrong. There has been a change in the time-lines, I can sense it. Something has happened in the past that has drastically affected this time-line."

Minister Gizelle conversed with his council members, they were checking computers, reading off in their native language. They were talking so fast that Robert and Jill could not believe it. It was like watching living computers, yet they were very much alive.

"Captain," Gizelle said. "We have found something. We must return to the home world, it is imperative that we reestablish our colony and for you to join us."

Chapter Eleven
The Reset Button?

Earth, 2105

Frank and Sara discussed the dilemma facing them all. They made the ultimate decision to wait things out, to give things time to play out. Frank could still feel his connection to the Centaurian people, and it was getting stronger. It was as if someone had hit a reset button on time and space. On the computer monitor, a news briefing was taking place.

"Would you look at that." Sara said, staring at the monitor. "I cannot believe that man is the leader of the world."

"Sadly, he plays a huge role in the future of humanity and will be the lead into something much worse." Frank said. "But, do not worry, if all goes well, things should take a turn. He is not the the one to worry about, however, his actions will play a huge role in everything."

"I don't understand. If he is not as bad as what is to come, why are you here now?"

"It is all together. This is the start of worse things to come, but there will come a time that will be calm for a while. I cannot go into full detail, for not even I am fully informed. All I know is this, I was sent here for a purpose. Humanity has reached a level of knowledge that they were not prepared for."

Sara sat quietly, looking at her bible lying on the table in front of her.

"You know," She said. "For millennia we have been taught that Jesus would return."

"Yes, I am aware of this teaching."

"For so many, they gave up hope. They stopped believing."

"Sadly, this is part of humanity. Only the *true* believers will endure and help to lead others."

"Are you saying that there is still hope?"

"There is always hope. I believe, as I was taught by my mother, that the bible speaks of faith. In fact, she would frequently say that 'faith is the substance of things hoped for and the evidence of things not seen,' she would say this to me many times in my life."

"Ah yes, Hebrews chapter eleven and verse one." Sara said as she opened her bible. "This is one of my favorite verses when I am feeling down or feel that things just aren't working out as planned."

"What are you two talking about?" Jean-Pierre asked as he returned from his walk.

"We were just --" Sara was cut off by her husband.

"Just doing some bible study it appears! We don't have time for any of this, we need to find answers!"

"The answers are here." Frank said, as he pointed to the bible.

"Nonsense!"

"Jean-Pierre, you need to sit down, shut up and listen!"

Shocked at his wife's assertiveness, he took a seat next to them as they brought him up to speed on everything.

"You know I am not a faith person Sara."

"You say this," Frank said. "However, that is not accurate. You do things by faith all the time."

"What do you mean?"

"When you are working on a new experiment, something that you are sure will work, it is in fact *faith* that you are experiencing. So, you do things by faith all the time."

Jean-Pierre scoffed. "Nonsense! It is not the same thing."

"Do you *hope* the experiment succeeds?"

"Of course, I hope all of my experiments are successful!"

"Then, it is *by faith* that you do this. 'Faith is the *substance* of things hoped for,' therefore, all that you do is done by faith."

Jean-Pierre sat with his lips perched tightly in anger at this discussion, sweat appeared upon his brow as the anger grew more intense.

"Why are you so upset?" Sara asked.

"None of this has anything to do with our current situation. I heard on the news, while listening to one of my audio books, as I was returning from my walk, that something was taking place and was leading to something major. People are beginning to rise up."

"Yes, I sense a change taking place. All things happen for a reason, that is what my mother always told me. Perhaps this was part of the Creator's will that I return to this time."

"Here we go again! Can we get through one discussion without you talking about some magical creator?"

Sara began to cry.

"Sara, my love, I am sorry. I should not have said that. I am just frustrated."

"As am I. But we must trust in our Lord to see us through this and have faith."

"Sara, you know I have a hard time with this. I don't know if there is a God or not. I know this, the universe and everything we see is too perfect to be just a random act. I do see a design."

"Yes, and to have design, there must be a designer." Frank added.

Frank was getting a more clear distinction of his connection to the time-lines. It was becoming clear to him that, as he was taught growing up, nothing happens that isn't part of the ultimate plan of the universe.

"Frank, are you okay?" Jean-Pierre asked. "You seem distant."

"I am fine. I am sensing my connection growing stronger. My time-line is becoming more clear."

"I am assuming," Sara said. "That the events are playing out more. The time-lines are resetting."

"Yes. My parents made contact, just as they should. Although, I do sense some changes, major changes, but they do not appear to have any affect on my role here."

"What about Faizan?" Jean-Pierre asked.

"I do not see the future as an open book. I can say this, there will be changes to come, if this time-line plays out as it should. I cannot however, tell you what those changes are. I will say this, keep your faith. You will need it."

"That sounds a little ominous." Sara said.

"Know this, things may get hard at times. But a better time is coming."

"Okay, so, you guys wanted to talk bible." Jean-Pierre said. "I have a question for you, my future grandson. The bible speaks of a return of the Messiah. For hundreds of years men preached to be ready, yet nothing. So, when? You seem to have all the answers."

Frank thought for a moment on how to respond. He was reminded of the Centaurian teachings on Earth history. He knew the stories. He knew the histories.

"Grandfather, as you know, I have learned a great deal from the Centaurian people; however, I do not have all the answers."

"That's the first time you have called me that."

"I know. I was unsure, I wasn't sure how you would react, considering everything that has happened."

"Okay, so what are we looking at?" Sara asked. "You said to keep the faith because we will need it."

"Again, I cannot see the exact future. As we have already seen here, the future is not yet fulfilled, therefore, things *can* change. I do know this, Faizan leads the way to a lot of changes on this world. I must meditate more and pray. Please excuse me."

♦

Prime Minister Akeem Faizan was staring coldly out his office window, swearing frequently. Still furious at the apparent traitor he had working under him.

At least I took care of those other traitors and their fleet of ships. He thought as he tapped on the large window pane in front of him.

"Prime Minister sir," A young man said as he entered the office. "I have some news regarding Sims."

"Really?" He asked, sarcastically. "What could you possibly tell me that I haven't already figured out."

"Sir, it appears --" He paused.

"It appears what? Come on boy, I don't have all day!"

"Well sir, as strange as this may sound. It appears he is not from here."

"Why is that strange? We have people from all over the world here."

"That's not what I mean sir. I mean, not from this world."

A silence filled the room as Faizan considered his next move. This was not news to him, as he had already suspected something was different about Sims.

"Explain." Faizan said.

"We have encountered intelligence that suggests that he may be from the Alpha Centauri system."

"A Centaurian? There have been no records of them for years. If this is true, I want him and his ship found."

"Yes sir."

A Centaurian, here -- This could be a problem

◆

Frank sat in the clearing meditating and praying. He knew things were about to get bad for this world, but was it his place to tell them their possible fate? Would they listen? Jean-Pierre was not a man that tends to believe such warnings. After all, people have been giving warnings of disaster and peril for years. Why would this be any different. Sara on the other hand, she was an open minded person. She might listen. Frank would spend the next two hours in prayer and meditation, seeking the right path before returning to the lab.

"Grandfather," Frank said as he returned. "We need to talk."

"Is something wrong?" Sara asked as they all gathered around the table.

"I am going to share a story, one that may seem hard for you to understand, so, please bare with me. It is important and the Creator, God, wants you to know these things before I leave."

"So, now you *talk* to God?" Jean-Pierre asked sarcastically.

"Not in the way that you and I talk. I believe Grandmother understands."

"You are talking about a spiritual connection." She said.

"Yes. You know the story in Genesis, the creation events. But, what you do not understand is there is a lot more to this story. So much more."

"If this is meant to be historically accurate texts, then why is there no evidence and why is it so vague?" Jean-Pierre was very skeptical and looked for anything to argue over when it came to science and history.

"Let me explain. As you know, I have a connection with the Centaurian people, who have a spiritual connection with God, as we know him. He is known by many names of course. In fact, he told Moses that he was 'I am That I Am' which in the ancient Hebrew tongue is translated as YAHWEH, or more precisely spelled as YHWH. This roughly is pronounced with the sound of breathing."

Frank continued to tell the story as it was told to him, to his grandparents, recounting all that he knew from his mother and from the Centaurian teachers. He recounted the creation story, but with a little more detail going back to the *beginning* with the first earth all the way to the creation of man. Sara was absorbing all that Frank was sharing, while Jean-Pierre was still questioning his story. Until --

"Now, let's talk aliens," Frank said. "In the bible, it is written that the 'sons of God took wives and bore children' and this was a race of giants. This is Genesis chapter six."

"What does that have to do with aliens?" Jean-Pierre asked.

"Hush and let him talk." Sara said, silencing her husband.

"For years, it was told that beings came from the heavens, and this was thought to be aliens. The fact was, while they were from another world, so to speak, and they were *alien* to man, they were in fact, fallen angels."

Jean-Pierre scoffed. "Fallen angels huh?"

"Yes, this goes back to the great war in Heaven. These beings were giants among men, gods even."

This now had the attention of his grandfather, who was now seeing a way to debate the creation and God.

"So, they were gods? This throws your entire theory of a single God out the door."

"No, there is only one *true* God and creator of this vast universe. These beings, though they were celestial, took on human form, saw the human females, finding them attractive, they took them as wives and their offspring became known as Nephilim, or giants. This led to the time of Noah and the flood."

Frank continued his bible lesson, hoping that he could lead his grandfather to God before he left. He talked into the morning hours, teaching and giving more than Sara had ever learned in her life, all thanks to the extra knowledge given to Frank through his Centaurian teachers.

Sara became so engrossed in her grandson's teachings. The fact that it had not been so long ago, that he was thought to be a traitor to them and was known by the name of Sims. Now, here he sat with an abundance of knowledge from the future. But why? What was so important that he had to tell them these things? Why now?

Jean-Pierre was slowly coming to an understanding. The way that Frank taught, the knowledge he shared. It was too detailed, too in depth. He was beginning to see why his wife of so many years felt the way she did, and now he was starting to feel sorrow for the many times he came against her when it came to the bible and God.

How could I have been so cruel to my lovely wife all these years? He thought to himself, as he continued to listen to Frank.

"When Jesus told his followers," Frank said, as he continued his lesson, "that he would return, they asked when? He gave them signs to watch for. Mankind has so ignorantly mistook this message and tried to predict his return. Jesus warned that no man or angel or even himself knew when he would be back. Only God. Remember when I said that heaven exists on a different plain of existence?"

"Yes." His grandparents answered in unison.

"Well, also remember that I said God's time frame was not ours. Grandfather, you know as a scientist that time is not as constant as we see it."

"You are correct. According to research, many factors can affect time. For example, traveling at the speed of light would theoretically stop time for the person who is traveling at that speed. However, we know that man cannot travel at light speed."

"Yes, that is one way. However, there is so much more to time and space that has yet to be discovered by mankind. God's realm, Heaven, is much more than what we see here. It is a spiritual realm that exists on an entirely different plain of existence. Another dimension, if that is more understandable for you. Time for God moves differently."

Frank continued to educate to the best of his abilities, he knew that the information he was sharing was important, not just for his grandparents, but for humanity. It was up to them as to how they would use this information.

Jean-Pierre listened intently as his future grandson shared this knowledge. He was still feeling skepticism, as a scientist, he would question everything. Looking for *evidence* to prove any theory. As he listened to Frank, his skepticism began to fade.

"I have question," Jean-Pierre began "if all of this is true, and I am not saying I believe, but if all of this is true. Then why is God allowing this to happen, why not just go back in time and stop it?"

"It is not that simple grandfather, although time moves in a different – well, it just moves differently. God doesn't just time travel and change history. In fact, the only reason I am here now, is because there were events that should not have happened. Now, we most try to fix those things."

"I think I understand, but I am still uncertain about all of this."

"I understand, grandfather, but we must move forward."

Frank continued his lesson on time dilatation and how this could affect so many things in the time-lines. He also tried to ex-plain the spiritual realms, and how time moved a different rates for the spirit realm than on earth.

"Frank," Sara interrupted, "you talked about the beginning, can you tell us more about that time period?"

"Perhaps another time. We have a lot of work ahead of us, and we must stay focused. I will say this, I believe, as people of science, that you understand more than you think."

"I know that, growing up, I was taught that the world and the universe was created in a short period of time. But, as I grew and learned more, I learned about the scientific creation. I always found myself questioning, and that made me feel as if I was denying my faith."

Frank was quiet for a moment, as he contemplated what his grandmother had just said.

"God created us with the ability to learn and he wanted us to be knowledgeable. Sadly, mankind took advantage of that. You however, have used your knowledge in a way to benefit man and to learn more about God. With that, I would say, you have nothing to be ashamed of or to worry about. You have not de-nied your faith."

Chapter Twelve
A Revelation
Alpha Centauri System, 2305

The Council of Centaur had successfully reached the other Centaurian people and many would be returning to their home world, Minister Gizelle had already begun the process of re-building their society. The satellites had been removed from or-bit and all evidence of humanity's destruction on their world had been erased. The Centaurians were capable of manipulating more than time and space. They also had the ability to manipu-late the environment. Their species were not only intelligent, but adaptive. They could survive harsh conditions that the average human could not.

To accommodate their new friends, changes had to be made to the planet's environment to allow humans to survive. With a few adjustments to the weather and the planetary artifi-cial bio-sphere, the atmospheric conditions would soon be safe for the crew to visit the surface. Currently, though there was oxy-gen, it was not at safe levels. Once completed, the remaining hu-mans could grow and learn from their new friends.

◆

"Robert," Jill said. "Do you think we will ever locate the rest of the fleet? I am really concerned that there could have been other saboteurs. I find it a bit odd that things have hap-pened this way, I mean with the time difference and all."

"I have thought about that a lot over the past few days while we have been waiting on the Centaurians to make the changes needed for us. I plan to question Ellis today."

"Do you think he will reveal if there were others?"

"I'm not sure, but I plan to try."

Jill stared out the window of the ready room. Her mind wondering as she thought about the events that have happened. An entire civilization was devastated because of humanity.

"I'm going to try to get some rest," Jill said. "The Centaurian council should be ready for us by 0900 hours."

"Good night. I think I will check on the ship status then get some rest myself. I think Ensign Orr can handle things."

Morning would come early for the crew. The Centaurians had stated that things should be ready at that time.

◆

Minister Gizelle and the Centaurian Ministry of Science worked to bring the new upgrades online. Centaur or Proxima b, as it was known by those on earth, was a tidally locked planet. Meaning, that one side was always facing it's home star. Usually consisting of a harsh climate, averaging a very cold environment, reaching temperatures as low as negative thirty-eight degrees Fahrenheit. Although it was a cold environment, the Centaurians were an adaptive race and could handle extreme weather.

Not completely inhabitable by humans of course, considering temperatures could reach those numbers or lower in certain areas on earth. In Alaska, winter can bring temperatures ranging from -30 to -35 degrees Fahrenheit while Siberia has seen temperatures as low as -78 degrees Fahrenheit. However, this planet was lacking in vegetation and animal life.

"Contact the captain," Gizelle said. "Tell him we are ready."

A message was sent to the Jean-Pierre, informing their guests that everything was ready. The average temperature was now a comfortable 70 degrees Fahrenheit. This would also allow the Centaurian people to adapt more quickly to the environmental changes.

◆

"Why did you do this?" Robert asked.

"You know why." Mark Ellis said. Sitting in the ship's brig he was much more humbled than when he attempted mutiny.

"You realize the predicament this places me in." Robert said.

"I do."

"This would be punishable by death back on earth under the current government leadership."

"I am aware."

"You are a man of few words aren't you?"

Ellis made direct eye contact with Robert, his glare was loud, while he remained silent. His message was clear.

"I'll deal with you later." Robert said as he turned to leave.

"You will not stop us." Ellis said, without looking up.

Robert paused, then continued to meet his first officer.

"How was your meeting with Ellis?" Jill asked, as they met in the corridor.

"Honestly? I am not sure. He was not talkative at all."

"What did he say?"

"Nothing really. And that worries me. I have dealt with men like him, cold and heartless. In fact, they usually worked as hit-men."

"What are we going to do?"

"If this was earth and under the current leadership, he would face a death sentence. Here? I am not sure. I am not ready to sentence someone to death."

"Perhaps the Centaurians have some type of rehabilitation they can offer."

"We will soon find out."

Captain Valentine and Commander Wright would both visit the planet's surface, along with their new security officer who would be replacing Mark Ellis. A young Lieutenant who had prior experience in security by the name of John Harris. They all met in the shuttle bay where they would take the shuttle craft Endurance to the surface.

"Lieutenant John Harris reporting for duty sir." He said as he stood at attention.

"At ease Lieutenant. Welcome to the team. I trust you have been briefed." Robert said.

"Aye Captain." He replied. "Sir, are we really going to meet an alien species?"

Robert laughed.

"Yes. I forgot many of you were still being brought out of stasis and were working below on ship systems." Robert said.

"I'm sorry sir, I did not mean --"

Robert stopped his new security chief "It is fine Harris, we are a long way from home. So, no worries. Let's go meet our new friends, after all, they just did a major change to their home just for us."

The three boarded the shuttle and departed for the surface. The Centaurian Ministry of Science had given them coordinates for entering the bio-sphere and where they were to land. A team would meet them there and escort them to meet with Minister Gizelle.

Jill entered the coordinates into the shuttle's navigation and turned controls over to the computer. From this point on, they were all just passengers.

"Anyone else nervous?" Jill asked, trying to break the silence.

"Are you?" Robert asked in response, avoiding that he was.

"What about you Harris?" Jill asked.

"A little." He answered. Visibly nervous.

"It is good to be a little nervous," Robert said. "After all, we are about to embark on a new mission to possibly colonize a planet that is already inhabited. So, basically, we will be coexisting with them."

The remainder of the time was quiet and short lived, as the trip only took around twenty minutes. They were to meet with the Ministry of Science here, then proceed to meet with their friend Minister Gizelle at the central command center that had been set up for the crew.

"We have arrived," Jill said as she took controls for final landing procedures. "Welcome to Proxima b, or as they refer to it, Centaur. The outside temperature is a cozy seventy degrees and the weather seems clear."

"Funny Jill. Very funny." Robert said.

"I thought I would lighten the mood some." She laughed.

The shuttle came to smooth stop at the coordinates given to them by the Centaurians. Robert, Jill and their new security chief, John Harris exited the shuttle to be greeted by three members of the Ministry of Science.

"Greetings. I am council member Gordash of the Ministry of Science."

"Greetings," Robert said, staring at the tall figure in front of him. "I apologize for staring, but you do not look like the others we have met."

"Indeed. We have the ability to take on other forms, it helps us to adapt to certain environments. We chose the human form. I hope you are not offended."

"Not at all, I apologize again, it was just a little bit of a shock."

"I assume," Jill said. "This is how your people interacted with humans in our past on earth."

"Yes, that is true. I am sure you have many questions."

Gordash led the trio to meet Minister Gizelle who was waiting in a nearby location. The surface of the planet was nothing like they expected. It was a barren land. Mountainous terrain with smooth cliff walls and plateaus surrounding the area. There was no evidence of life outside of what they were seeing in front of them.

"Do you see this?" Jill asked in a whisper to Robert.

"Indeed," He whispered. "If I did not see life with my own eyes, I would say this planet was uninhabitable."

Lieutenant Harris interrupted the other-wise silent walk. "May I ask a question?"

"Sure." Gordash replied.

"Where are the buildings?"

Robert glanced at Jill, knowing they had the same question.

"You shall soon see." Gordash answered as they kept walking.

He led them to a nearby cliff wall, which appeared to be solid stone with a smooth surface. Robert reached out, touching the surface.

"It's as smooth as glass." He said.

"So, are we on a geological tour here?" Jill asked.

"Not exactly." Gordash raised his arm and waived gently in front of the wall. The seemingly solid surface faded and opened into a room filled with equipment.

Entering the room, they could see all forms of highly advanced technology. The wall they just entered through had solidified once again, only this time it was now semi-transparent. Other members of the Ministry of Science were working diligently at stations throughout the massive room.

"What is this place?" Robert asked.

"This is our operations and research center. Here we maintain the bio-sphere and monitor the space-time continuum. We can monitor any of our teams who are traveling to other worlds or time-lines." Gordash explained.

"What exactly happened with that wall?" Jill asked.

"We have the ability to manipulate matter, as you witnessed when Council Minister Gizelle arrived on your ship. The wall is actually a hologram."

"But it was solid, I could touch it." Robert said.

"Indeed. With the ability to manipulate matter, we can create holographic projections that have mass."

This was something out of twentieth century science fiction on earth. Robert remembered however, that researchers had been experimenting with a type of holographic technology before the wars began.

"Where is Minister Gizelle?"

"He will be joining us shortly captain. Until then, feel free to look around. If you have any questions, we will be happy to assist and answer as we are permitted by the council."

"I understand," Robert said. "This is a lot of tech to keep safe and I would be the same way."

"I have a few questions," Harris said. "What about security? I mean you were almost wiped out because of a lack of security. I mean this with the utmost respect of course."

"A valid question." Jill said.

"Ah yes," Gordash said as he led the trio to a nearby station that had several star systems showing on the monitors. "Here you will see the latest in advanced monitoring. This allows us to detect any threat within half of a parsec or approximately a little over a light year away. Considering --" He paused.

"Considering what?" Robert asked.

"I will allow Minister Gizelle to continue explaining. Until then, let me show you our food replication system. As you have noticed, I am sure, the planet has no vegetation. We Centaurians are capable of survival with nutritional supplements. However, we are aware that humans require more, those requirements in mind, we created this to accommodate your needs."

Just what I was looking forward to. Fake food. Robert thought.

"Minister Gizelle will join you shortly. I must go now, I have work to complete on the environmental accommodations."

The trio sat at a large round table that sat off to the far side of the room, lab or whatever it was they were in. Robert sat quiet, he was feeling uneasy about something, but wasn't sure what was bothering him. Jill and Lieutenant Harris talked security details and crew rosters. They wanted to maintain an active orbit even after their new co-colonization begins.

"Welcome to Centaur, or as you know it, Proxima b. I hope you have taken the time to look around."

The voice was that of Minister Gizelle, however, the person standing before them was a tall blonde man with crystal blue eyes and a light complexion. He was dressed in his council robes, however, underneath was clearly an earth style suit and tie.

"Minister Gizelle?" Robert asked, clearly unsure if it was him.

"Yes. This is the form I took when I visited earth many years ago. I grew rather fond of it."

"I'm sorry, I don't mean to stare. It's just, well, you look like the description of someone from stories of alien-beings during the early twentieth century." Robert said.

"I am sure. Many of our people took similar forms."

"I am not sure I understand," Jill said. "Your people are willing to change their lives and appearance to benefit us?"

"As I have stated many times now commander, we are a very peaceful race. We only wish to help, as we always have. Now that you have achieved deep space travel and the ability to create wormholes, we can now show you more than you currently know."

"Minister." One of the science members called out.

They talked quietly for a moment, the one who called out seemed to be concerned or even upset about something. Minister Gizelle was clearly showing concern.

"Jill, look, something is up over there." Robert said.

"I noticed."

"I can try to get a closer look and listen." Harris said.

"No, you should wait here. Jill and I will find out what is up."

Gizelle began to walk back towards the table. A definite look of concern was upon his new-found human face and he clearly was unable to hide it.

"Is something wrong minister?" Robert asked.

"Captain, I must talk to you. In private."

Gizelle guided Robert into a nearby room, also hidden by a holographic wall. The two sat at a small round table, it appeared to be a small conference room or perhaps a study. There were scrolls displayed on shelves on either side of the room and a small computer console of some type sitting on a nearby desk.

"Captain, I wanted to talk in private to discuss the wormhole you traveled through."

"Sure, what do want to know about it?"

"How much do you know about the creation of the first?"

"The first? I am not sure I am following you minister."

"The first wormhole. The one that was created in the lab so long ago when your father first discovered the particle."

"No, no. It wasn't like that at all. When he first discovered the stable particle several years went by before more experiments took place."

"What can you tell me about that time?"

Robert thought for a moment, remembering the events of that time. The things that had led to the creation of the fleet.

"Well. I remember the stories, that my father had discovered a stable version of the so-called God Particle. In fact, he told me once about a man, a man that one day I would meet, who would save the world. I thought it was just a story."

"Do you know why the mission was started?"

"No. Only that he had been instructed to work on a project that was top-secret. I later learned it would involve space travel."

"Indeed. There was actually a lot more to this story though. Wasn't there?"

"Yes. After the creation of the fleet. We were informed of the details that would lead to the *Project Wormhole* program. And from there, all I recall was the rush to push the program ahead by one year."

Gizelle was quiet for a moment before responding.

"Do you recall the reason for the early launch?"

"Yes. The world was facing a ruthless leader who wanted to control everyone. He wanted to control the population by --"

"By what? Take your time, but it is important that I know all that you know of this mission."

"He wanted to commit genocide. From there, a man named Sims was working with my father and my team on what we now knew as *Project Wormhole*."

"That's it. That is the missing detail."

"Project Wormhole?"

"No. Sims. I can't tell you anything further, it could severely contaminate the time-line."

Gizelle ended their conversation and left the room. A look of concern still on his face and *that* concerned Robert. He went back to join the others, not sure if he should tell them or not of the conversation. The only thing that he could think of right now, was that look on Gizelle's face. Something was not right, and that made him feel very uneasy.

Chapter Thirteen

Enlightenment

Earth, 2105

Jean-Pierre sat in his study, thinking about the things Frank had told them. About time, space, other dimensions and God. He sat there at his little desk for over two hours. On the desk was the bible Sara was looking at while they were talking. It was still open to the last scripture she was reading. Genesis chapter one.

The words that Frank had spoken regarding God's time and man's time were winding through his thoughts. As a physicist who had studied multiple theories regarding the multiverse and other dimensional theories, this was intriguing to him. Could God be real? Could there be beings in another dimension with the ability to move along the space-time continuum at will? Did a being with supernatural powers really create everything known to man, including mankind? So many questions were rolling through his mind at this point.

"Jean-Pierre, are you okay?"

Startled, he replied. "Yes my love, I am just thinking."

"Do you want to talk?"

"Not right now. I think we need to consider at this point all of the possibilities before us."

"You believe him, don't you?"

"I am not sure what I believe, but I know this. He knows too much and we have already seen the advanced tech he has. I mean, I don't know if his praying is a communication with God or not."

"You know, you are just looking at this the wrong way Jean-Pierre. Stop being so scientific."

This was something that Jean-Pierre always had issues with. Science was his life, it is who he is. Years of research, study and he had never taken the time to listen to his wife. The things that Frank had said made sense in so many ways. He knew one thing for sure -- the world was in chaos and something had to change.

◆

Frank stared off into the stars, deep in thought. He knew he had to do something to set things right. The plan was to go back and save humanity. Instead, it appears he may have made things worse. He could sense his mentor stronger each day, which could only mean that the time-lines were intact. No major changes took place to alter his family.

What else has changed because of me? What have I done?

Frank's thoughts filled his mind. Not noticing his grandmother standing nearby.

"Frank. Are you okay?"

"Oh, hi. Yes, I am fine. I was just thinking about all of this and what I have --" He paused before continuing, not sure of his next words. "Look, I have to be honest. My father, your son, would have made this trip anyway, with or without my help. The fact is, grandfather was already on the verge of discovering all of this before I arrived. But --"

"What is it Frank? What is bothering you?"

"What if I am the cause of so many people dying? The things I saw in my connection with the time-line, the destruction to the Centaurian home world. What if I am the cause of it all?"

Sara thought for a moment before answering.

"Look, I do not understand all there is to know about this. I do know this. I believe that all things happen for a purpose."

"I suppose that is one way of thinking. But, when I left, all was fine. The Jean-Pierre was safe, albeit in the future by two hundred years. I thought I could change that, perhaps change history to save all of humanity. My mission was to save you and grandfather while possibly stopping Faizan at the same time."

"Wait," Jean-Pierre said as he joined Frank and Sara. "You came back to save us? I thought your primary mission was to stop Faizan and to launch the mission early."

"There is so much I did not or rather cannot tell you."

"Let me guess, it may cause a paradox?"

"Not really," Sara said. "Not a paradox, but knowing too much could jeopardize a lot, including our lives."

"Exactly. That is why I must be cautious in what I say or do."

"I hate time travel."

Jean-Pierre's statement made Sara chuckle a bit, but she could understand his feelings. Time travel has always been something that fascinated her though, so this was definitely something she could understand.

"Let me see if I can explain without revealing too much detail and risking contamination of the time-line."

Frank thought for a moment before continuing.

"When I came here, my objective was to stop the madness that Faizan had created. When the new one world government came into existence, Faizan was not the mad man you see now. He --"

Frank paused, not sure if he should share more than what he has already. Too much detail could prove just as harmful if not more harmful than what he has already done. But he knew he had to tell them about the mission and why it was so important.

"He what?" Jean-Pierre asked.

"He was influenced."

"By whom?" Sara asked, now even more intrigued.

Frank was silent for a moment as he thought more about how to proceed with his revelation.

"Come on boy, spit it out, let's here it. Sara and I aren't getting any younger here. Who was he influenced by?"

"All I can say is, the Centaurians aren't the only alien-beings."

"Are you saying that he is under the influence of aliens or is he an alien?" Sara asked.

"No. He is human, but, he is being controlled through alien technology. That is why I am here, or one reason. I came to stop him. When I discovered I was unable to do so, I had to find a new way to save you. It all started *before* you made your discovery. Faizan had not become the leader of the new government yet."

Frank told them everything he could without revealing too much detail. He had been to earth before the time he first met his grandfather in the lab. Faizan was set to become the new leader of the New United Nations and the one world movement. At first, he was a man of peace. However, that all changed when he met a man who promised him a way to change the world.

He was presented with technology that he had never seen. A technology that was more advanced than anything on earth. All he had to do was to merge with it, becoming one with this organic tech that would change him forever.

"When he merged with this alien technology, it altered his mind and his DNA. He became part of it. He was now set to rule this world. I can say this, the species that he joined is more than anything you could imagine. And that is all I can say."

"Let me get this straight," Jean-Pierre said. "Faizan is an alien now?"

"Not exactly," Sara said. "I think he is being controlled by an alien technology."

"More like he has become one with the alien tech. It is hard to explain, and I cannot go into a lot of detail. But know this, all of the things happening will lead to --"

He paused. He knew he needed to tell them more, but he also new he had to keep a lot to himself. If he reveals too much, it could alter the time-line in irreparable ways. If he did not reveal enough, he may not be able to fix what he has already caused.

"What will it lead to Frank?" Sara asked.

"Please understand. I cannot reveal too much. You understand why. You above all people know what contaminating the time-lines can cause."

"Well, I know this. Something has to change. We cannot just sit here and do nothing." Jean-Pierre said. "Isn't there some alien tech that you have access to?"

"I understand what you are saying grandfather, but the aliens we work with are a peaceful race with no weapons. They depend of faith to get them through."

Jean-Pierre scoffed.

"Here we go with the *faith* line again."

"Pay no attention to your stubborn grandfather Frank. But, in all seriousness, what can we do?"

"It is possible that things can be turned around. In fact, I know it will. But, at the same time, lives will be lost. I am not sure I can prevent that, or if I should. Even saving a life could alter things to the worse."

"I agree. As horrible as it sounds. You could save a life that in the end could have been someone who would be worse than who we have now." Jean-Pierre said.

Sara thought for a moment before responding to her husband. Although he was close in his understanding. Saving a life, that could do more, as *that* could create a paradox event. In fact, saving the Valentines was a risk, however, it appears it was a risk worth taking.

"I suppose you could look at it in that way," Frank said. "But it is more than that."

"A paradox event." Sara said, almost in a whisper.

"Yes. That is the main concern. We have already witnessed a major change in the time-lines. Thankfully it appears to be correcting itself along the way. But at what loss? I need to pray a while."

"Pray? At a time like this?"

Jean-Pierre huffed. Although he was understanding more and more about faith, he was still a little agnostic about the matter.

"Let him be." Sara said.

◆

Frank sat under the star lit sky, staring off into the vastness of its beauty. He could name each star he could see. Out there in all that vastness was his family and friends. He was missing them.

He cleared his mind and began to meditate and pray. Focusing his thoughts on the Creator of the universe and all that is seen. He prayed for the knowledge he needed to choose the right path. How much should he reveal and how much would they believe? His family, when he left them, had grown closer to the Creator and was living in peace among the Centaurians. Their faith had grown so much. Now, with the changes that have taken place, he wondered if that all was the same.

As he meditated he could feel his connection to the timelines and he could sense changes that were taking place. Some good and some bad. He was uncertain of which of those feelings involved his family and that concerned him.

Chapter Fourteen
A New Life Begins
The Planet Centaur, 2325

It had been twenty five years since the Jean-Pierre arrived in the Alpha Centauri system and made contact with the Centaurian people. A full colony had been established on the planet known previously as Proxima b, and now as Centauri. Now married, Robert and Jill were the leaders of mankind in space. Learning more about the universe and earth history than they could ever imagine. Jill was nine months pregnant, and due to give birth at anytime to their son.

"Jill, you need to rest."

"Robert, you are always such a worrier. I'll be fine, the doctor said it could be a few days before the baby comes. Besides, we have some of the best medical care in the galaxy."

"Yeah, the Centaurians have been wonderful to us. I am so glad that things worked out the way that it did. Not to mention the fact we located the rest of the fleet."

The remainder of the fleet was located about one light year away over ten years ago after the Jean-Pierre arrived. All of the crew members were still in stasis and safely brought out once the ships were located. Now, they were on new missions, with each ship assigned to different quadrants of the galaxy.

"The upgrades to all of the ships will definitely help with the deep space exploration." Jill said.

"Definitely. Not to mention the upgrades taking place to the Jean-Pierre, making it the flag ship of the future."

Jill wrenched in pain.

"Are you okay?" Robert asked, taking her by the hand.

"You better call Doctor Kyros."

Robert called for the doctor, his wife now in labor. He waited patiently for the arrival of his son, thinking about their lives now, living in space and on another planet.

I cannot believe I am about to become a father. I wish mom and dad were here to meet their grandson.

"Captain Valentine, it is time." Dr. Kyros said.

Jill was in labor for a short period of time thanks in part to the medical advancements of the Centaurians. She gave birth to a healthy boy, they named Frank Jean-Pierre Valentine. Frank would be the first human born on another world and would lead to advancements in human DNA. The unique environment he would be subjected to would allow him to develop a strong and somewhat superior muscular skeletal system compared to other humans.

"Captain, you and your wife have a special child here. A child that will undoubtedly become a leader in his own rights as the years pass." Minister Gizelle stated as he joined them at the med center.

"The doctor tells us that he already exhibits advancements in his DNA compared to Robert and I."

Gizelle could see the look of concern on Jill's face.

"No need to worry commander. Your child is healthy and will develop just fine."

◆

Several months had passed since the birth of Frank. He was already showing a high-level of intelligence. He began to walk at the early age of six months and was using complete sentences before he reached ten months of age. Gizelle was already working with him on his education, based on his eagerness to learn new things. He was certain that young Frank would do amazing things for the human race.

"Robert, I cannot believe how intelligent Frank is."

"Of course he is! He has our DNA."

They both chuckled at his failed attempt at making a joke. The fact remained, that Frank was developing much faster than either parent had expected. They were only a few days from celebrating Frank's first birthday and he was already talking well beyond his age. Using complete phrases, with proper syntax nonetheless.

The Valentines Centaurian home was created from the same high-tech materials as the science lab they had encountered when they first arrived. It was a split level design, with an earthly feel to it. Jill helped the science team with the designs using images from her personal files. The lower level of their home consisted of an office space on the far side that was easily separated by the same holographic wall technology as the lab. The family area of the home had interactive hologram projectors that allowed for the family to create any scenario they could want.

On the far wall of the lower level, there were consoles, each one with separate operations. Including food replication. On the upper level were the sleeping quarters, which consisted of three separate quarters, each with their own *personal care stations* or bath rooms.

Door Chimes

"Come in." Jill said.

"Greetings my friends," Minister Gizelle said as he entered their home. "I hope I am not intruding."

"Not at all," Robert said. "Please, come in."

"How is our young friend today?"

"See for your self," Robert said, motioning towards Frank who was interacting with a holographic Albert Einstein. "He found this program and has been at it ever since."

"He is reading now?" Gizelle asked, as he pointed out a book lying open on the table beside Frank.

"No, at least not that we know of. However, Frank is doing things everyday that surprises us." Jill said, as she sat down with a cup of freshly replicated tea. "Just like this program. He simply stated to the computer that he wanted to learn more about science. I guess it pulled from our earth records and created this."

"Fascinating. He is developing much quicker than anticipated, much quicker indeed."

The Valentines looked at each other with concern hearing this. What did he mean *anticipated* and why were the Centaurians so interested in his development?

"Minister," Robert said. "I don't understand. You said that he is developing faster than you anticipated. What do you mean?"

"Please, let me explain. As you know, the conditions here on Centaur are much different than that of your home world and this has contributed to the faster than usual development of your son. We have been monitoring his growth for his own safety, and have learned a great deal about him in the process."

"Okay, but that still doesn't answer Robert's question. I think we need to know more about why you are monitoring our son."

Gizelle could sense the concern in Jill's voice and knew he had to ease her fears.

"Commander, please hear me out. Frank is a very special boy. Not only is he the first human born on another world, he also has a gift. The unique conditions have contributed to his growth in so many ways. Including his cognitive growth. Allowing him to accumulate knowledge at a much higher rate than others."

"So, our son is a genius." Robert said.

"You could say that, however, I would consider him a genetic *super human*. In other words, he is much stronger and dare I say, much more intelligent."

Neither parent spoke, they just listened inventively.

"Let me explain," Gizelle continued. "As I said, the uniqueness of the conditions here on Centaur will lead to the human body adapting. You yourselves will see this over time, however,

Frank and any other child will experience this adaptation much sooner."

"So, we are evolving?" Robert asked.

"No. Adapting. To evolve, a species would need to undergo major changes, basically becoming an entirely new species. That my friends contradicts the Creator's master plan."

"Speaking of the Creator. We have been here twenty-five years now. You promised several times that you would tell us more about how your people know so much of creation, spirituality and the human race." Jill said.

"Indeed, I did. Many millions of years ago the Creator of all things, that we are and see, created this universe. As you know; there are multiple dimensions, all created by the Creator. He chose to create this universe, in this dimension. It was a void in space and time. Perfect for all that we see. In the beginning, he created the universe that he allowed to grow until it reached the time for his ultimate creations. Life. While there are many species in the universe, most are of – shall we say, lesser intelligence?"

Gizelle shared a remarkable story of the ultimate creation period that lasted into the late hours. All leading up to the creation of our galaxy and life as we know it. Robert and Jill sat listening as he spoke. Frank also listened, but none of them saw him as he sat nearby, taking in everything that was being said. He was engrossed in the conversation.

"Wow, I have never heard the creation story like this." Jill said.

"I agree, I have heard the six days of creation and the day of rest, etc., but never this detailed back story." Robert added.

"The human race has always had difficulties with history and facts." Gizelle said, continuing his lesson. "After the Creator saw that the universe was at the level he desired, he chose to create this galaxy."

Hours went by as he described, in detail, the galactic creation period leading up to the creation of Earth and the other planets. He talked about the sun and the important role it played in all of the creation story-line. Then, he revealed something they were not expecting –

"My species was privileged to see this portion of the creation. Albeit from our home world; my people were given a special opportunity to view all of this as it happened. We waited until all was ready and then made our way into this dimension."

"Wait. You are not from this dimension? Are you from the same realm as God? Are you --" Jill paused mid sentence.

"No. There are multiple dimensions, all a part of the Creator's master work. We are from a dimension inhabited by a peaceful race of beings. We chose millions of years ago, your time, to live in harmony and peace. We are not supernatural beings, such as those in the realm and kingdom of the Creator. Rather, we are a part of his vast dimensional master design."

"But, you have a connection, a spiritual connection with God, right?" Robert asked.

"Yes, but no more than you yourselves can have."

Gizelle continued his lesson, telling how the solar systems came to be, the difference in time-lines in regards to the creation periods taught on earth. He also taught about the prehistoric times with dinosaurs, ice ages, and the destruction that led to the extinction of them and *why* God would allow his creation to be destroyed. Then, the big story – the creation of mankind and the world as we know it now.

"I was created." A young voice said, breaking the lesson.

"Frank?" Robert asked in awe of his young son's statement.

"I was created," he said again. "We all were created."

"Yes son, we are all part of creation." Jill said.

"No. I am created different."

Robert shot a look of amazement to Jill as they listened to their son speaking with such intelligence and with almost perfect understanding of sentence structure. How could a child so young have such intelligence?

Frank began to tell them more, saying that he understood that he was different, that he had an understanding of things that no others could comprehend. He was now forming full sentences and using words that were well beyond his age. Minister Gizelle found this very intriguing and wanted to hear more.

"May I ask him some questions?" Gizelle made sure to ask his parents before approaching the young boy with questions.

"Sure." Jill answered.

"Frank, do you know who I am?"

"Yes." Frank answered. "You are Minister Gizelle Oorurah of the Council of Centaur."

Astonished at their son's speech and knowledge, Robert and Jill became suspicious. How could a child so young develop such intelligence? Did the Centaurian people do something to him?

"This is crazy," Robert said. "A child this age should barely be speaking, but my son is not only speaking, he knows things well beyond his age!"

Jill began to cry.

"Please," Gizelle began. "Don't be upset commander. You can be proud, your son has a gift of knowledge. We can only assume the conditions of this world may be a contributing factor."

"You did this to him, didn't you?" Robert asked in anger.

"No. I assure you, we did nothing. We too are astonished at his development."

"So, again, you're saying our son is a genius." Jill said, as she wiped away tears.

"As I stated before, you could say that. Frank is a gifted child with a great future ahead."

Minister Gizelle continued to question Frank and watch his actions. While he had toys to play with, he chose the complexity of puzzles. He was also fascinated with numbers and the stars.

"Robert. Jill. As you can see, your son has a gift and that gift should be nurtured."

"I agree." Jill said.

"As do I." Robert added.

"I would like to offer Frank a chance to learn more. We would like to begin at once with his full education. If that is acceptable."

Silence filled the room as the Valentines contemplated things. On one hand, the Centaurians could offer a lot more in education with their advanced development and knowledge. On the other, would they be taking away their son's child-hood?

They came to a decision. They would allow Frank to choose.

"Frank dear, come here a moment. Your dad and I have a question for you."

"Yes mom?"

"Frank," Robert said. "Minster Gizelle would like to offer you a chance to attend a special school where you can learn more."

"Okay." Frank said.

"Frank, we would like for you to attend class with some of our young scholars here on Centaur. Would you like that?"

"I would love to!"

"Wonderful. You can start whenever you like."

"Really? Can I start now dad?"

"If you want to son, it is okay with your mom and I."

"Then it is settled. Frank will begin classes tomorrow. I'll come by and personally escort him to and from class."

♦

Frank would attend classes over the next several weeks. Each day learning new and exciting things to share with his parents.

"Robert, do you think we did the right thing?"

"I ask myself that every day. But, Frank seems happy and he is learning a lot. How many one year old children do you know who can read fluently and complete complex mathematical equations? Heck, he read me a story last night, from Shakespeare."

Frank would continue learning, gaining more knowledge each day. He would continue his education over the next several months until –

"Mom. Dad. May I ask a question?"

"Sure son." Robert replied.

"What happened to our family?"

"What do you mean?" Jill asked.

"My grandparents and all of the others left behind on earth."

"Well," Robert began. "We left earth in the year 2105, I'm sure we have some descendants from our family on earth. But, as for your grandparents --"

He paused, not sure what to say at this point. Frank was a very intelligent child, but he is still very young. How was he to tell him that they left behind his grandparents and all of the others.

"I know they are not alive now," Frank said. "But I'm curious about them and what happened."

Robert and Jill did their best to explain the events that led to the mission and their current time difference as to how they left earth over two hundred years ago, yet they were all still young. At least in appearance. This left their young son with more questions and he was determined to learn all he could.

The Valentines decided to invite Minister Gizelle to help them explain a few things. Only to learn that Frank was already aware of the wars that took place and the events that led to our mission. However, there were some things that he did not know.

♦

"Good evening Minister Gizelle, please come in." Jill said.

"Good evening commander."

"Frank has some questions, that Robert and I can't answer."

"Understood. However, before I talk to him, we need to talk."

Robert led their guest into the office area of their home where they could talk in private. He sent young Frank to his quarters to study late earth history.

"Captain. Commander. As you are aware, Frank has developed much faster than any of us expected. He is learning so much. We are now in his fourth earth month of learning. His advancement has taken the instructors to an all new level of instruction."

"Yes, we too are very surprised. His mother and I have grown concerned.

"No need to be concerned. Your son is an amazing young boy who has a mind for knowledge and I am sure he has many more questions. However, I --" He paused.

"You what?" Robert asked.

"Captain, I feel Frank is the perfect candidate for our latest bio-technology."

"I'm sorry, bio-technology?"

"Yes, it is a specialized microchip, a bio-chip. It will allow Frank to access his full potential as a Centaur born human. He is already exhibiting multiple skills that are well beyond that of any human child in history. This technology would allow him to do so much for humanity."

"Wouldn't this go against God and creation?" Jill asked.

"I understand your concerns commander. Please, rest assured we are not attempting to outdo the Creator in anyway. We give him all the honor in regards to your son's abilities. All we want is to offer young Frank a way to access his full potential and to use his gifts to help humanity."

"What would this microchip do?" Robert asked.

Gizelle went to the computer console, opening a file for Robert and Jill. On the monitor was an image of a microchip with a text box next to it. A combination of Centaurian language and English.

"Here you can see that the chip is very small, it would be a minimal procedure to implant. Of course, Frank would not feel it or even know it was there. The chip would allow him to develop more strength and intelligence by tapping into his neuromuscular systems. He would also gain access to extrasensory perception."

"Wait," Jill said. "ESP? Why would he need that?"

"All sentient beings have the ability to perceive more of their surroundings with extrasensory perception. Sadly, not everyone has learned how to access it. This will allow Frank to access his abilities that are a part of him."

"You said he could use this to help humanity. I am not sure I understand." Robert said.

"Humanity as a whole is in danger. You know that. However, I feel that humanity has strayed far away from the Creator and I believe Frank is the answer to help redirect them."

"How? He is only a child." Jill said.

"This will take time. Frank still has a lot to learn. He may be a very intelligent child, but he still needs to grow, learn and develop his abilities. This technology we are offering Frank will help him to achieve this."

"His mother and I will have to think about this. Your people has done so much for us over the years since we arrived. Even after all that happened. I believe you have Frank's best interest in mind."

"Please do. Understand this though, for this to work we need to begin with the procedure as soon as possible. I cannot go into details, but I must stress that Humanity will depend on Frank."

◆

"Robert, this is so hard. How do we decide to give our child an implant?"

"I know. I am not sure what to think about all of this, but I know that the Centaurians have been honest with us and they have proven time and time again that they hold our health and well-being at high standards."

"The part I do not understand is the saving humanity. How is Frank supposed to save humanity?"

"Good question. I think we should allow it."

"Maybe we should ask Frank." Jill said as she called their son into the room.

"I agree."

"Yes mom, you called for me?"

"Frank, your father and I need to talk to you for a moment. I know you are a very intelligent child. You understand so much. I want to ask you a question."

"Okay. What is it?"

"Minister Gizelle came to see us. He wants to offer you a way to learn even more." Robert said.

"However," Jill added. "This would mean that you would need to have a microchip. You know what that is, right?"

"Yes, we have been studying computer technology in school."

Robert looked at Jill in awe of his young child talking with such intelligence.

"Good. Minister Gizelle has asked your father and I about you having a special chip placed in your body. It would give you access to more learning. It would also make you stronger."

"So, your mother and I decided that you should be the one to decide if you want this or not."

Frank sat quiet for a moment, thinking about this offer. A way for him to learn more was intriguing to him and something that he felt was part of his future.

"Yes. I will allow them to do this."

Chapter Fifteen
A New Memory
Earth, 2105

Frank awoke early. While waiting on his grandparents to wake, he went out to the clearing to meditate under the stars. He felt something different, something new.

Something has changed. He thought.

"Good morning." Frank was startled by his grandfather's greeting.

"Good morning grandfather. I trust you slept well."

"Not really. How are you this morning?"

"I am unsure. Something is different today, something new. I am not sure what it is. I just --" Frank stopped, clutching his head he fell to his knees in pain.

"Frank! What's wrong?"

He did not answer.

"Frank!" Jean-Pierre continued to call out to his grandson.

"What's going on?" Sara asked as she ran to her husband.

"I don't know. He just grabbed his head and fell to his knees. He was saying that he felt something was different. Then this happened."

Frank stood slowly, massaging his temples.

"What happened?" Jean-Pierre asked.

"I am not sure. I felt a sudden pain in my head."

"You said something about something being different," Sara said. "Can you tell us more?"

"It was as if a flood of memories appeared at once."

"What type of memories?" Jean-Pierre asked.

"Memories from my child-hood. It appears the time-lines have reset now. I can sense much more."

"Your child-hood? Does that mean something changed in it or is it something more familiar?" Sara asked.

"It is difficult to explain. The memories are familiar, however, there are some subtle changes. But I cannot explain. I need to clear my thoughts and meditate a little more."

"Perhaps one of us should sit with you." Sara said.

"Your grandmother is right, I will sit with you."

"Very well, but please, I require complete silence."

Sara went back to the lab. She wanted to research a few things on temporal mechanics. It was apparent something had changed in future events that was affecting Frank. The question was, what was that change? Would that change make a difference in his mission?

Subtle changes? What could be subtle yet cause him to suffer sudden pain?

She continued her research, finding nothing substantial to explain what Frank was feeling.

"Sara, Frank has learned something." Jean-Pierre said as he and his grandson entered the lab.

"The time-lines have reset. I can now sense everything more clearly. It is time for me to return home. However, I need to talk with you, to tell you some things of importance."

"Frank, you know you cannot reveal too many things to us. It could be dangerous to the future. Your grandfather and I will be okay."

"No, you do not understand. It is part of my mission. What I need to tell you is why I returned."

Frank sat down with this grandparents, informing them of all he knew that was important to saving humanity from total chaos and destruction. They were the key. They, along with others who were already working, hold the key to saving the world.

"I am not sure I understand," Sara said. "As a person of faith, I find this to be outside of the scriptures."

"Indeed. The fact of the matter remains, a chain of events has taken place that should not have. Unfortunately, the discoveries made with the CERN projects led others to notice earth."

"Aliens?" Jean-Pierre asked, almost with a smirk, knowing how his grandson was carrying alien technology in his body.

"As you know, the Centaurian people have visited earth many times over the years. They are not the only visitors though. Some came and observed, waiting for the day that the particle was fully discovered and active."

"That sounds as if they were time travelers also." Sara said.

"No. They were here on earth when it was first discovered. They knew the potential it held and wanted to see just how far humanity would go with it."

"So, when I discovered the stable particle --"

"That got their attention. You set forth a chain of events that led to me being here now. As I said, you would have eventually found a way to create the wormhole yourself within the next year. In doing so, because you would lack the element needed to keep it stable, disaster would follow."

"That is why you returned, to stop me from creating it."

"Not entirely, I came back to stop the destruction and to help you to create a stable wormhole. Faizan was not originally part of my mission, he became a secondary mission because of influence from the other aliens."

"So what are we looking at now?" Sara asked.

"We need to repair the damage set forth without causing any more harm to the time-lines. Your mission is to get those who are rising up against Faizan to realize he is being influenced by aliens."

"We will need proof." Jean-Pierre said.

"Indeed, and I plan to give it to you."

Frank continued to give details regarding his plan, including how he would be able to obtain the proof needed. Now that the time-lines have reset he now had full access to his biotechnology that would allow him to achieve more than he had been.

"So, just how do you plan to get this proof?" Sara asked.

"As I stated, the proof I need will require a trip to Egypt."

"Exactly. As you can clearly see, I do not have access to a plane or other means to travel that far." Jean-Pierre said.

"Now that I have full access to the biotechnology, I also have access to my transporter. Now am I able to travel through time and space, I also have the ability to transport across long distances while on earth."

An alert came across the alert system.

"Faizan," Sara said. "What is he up to now"

On the screen, the prime minister was about to speak.

"Citizens of One World Earth, today marks a new era in our world. Thanks to a physicist by the name of Jean-Pierre Valentine, we have seen the creation of a stable wormhole that will allow for deep space travel. Sadly, Dr. Valentine and his partner have stolen this technology --"

"What!? How dare he accuse me of that!"

"I am offering a reward for his capture and the return of this technology to the New United Nations. This technology needs to be returned, at *any* cost. Use what ever means necessary to return the technology."

"No, this cannot happen. It is not suppose to happen. I am failing my mission. If he gains access to the wormhole he will cause the ultimate destruction. Without the element --"

"What element?" Sara asked.

"Element X. It is the element found on Centaur that allows for the stable wormhole. It is only stable on earth for a short period. As of now, the element is already becoming unstable. Without that element, if he attempts to open a wormhole --"

"Disaster." Jean-Pierre finished his grandson's statement.

"Exactly." Frank said.

"What can we do now?" Sara asked.

"I am not sure. I know this, it is imperative now that I retrieve the item in Egypt. With that, you will have the proof that will allow you to lead a revolution against Faizan and stop him from causing more chaos. The faith must be restored."

"Again with the faith --"

"Not now Jean-Pierre!" Sara scolded.

"I must go now, I will return shortly. I have something I need to do first before I go to Egypt."

Frank closed his eyes, concentrating and then, he began to fade into what appeared to be light filled particles. He was gone in only a few seconds.

"Now I am officially going crazy in my old age." Sara said.

"I wonder what he meant? He is up to something I just know it." Jean-Pierre said.

♦

Prime Minister Faizan paced in his office, as he waited for his reward of Jean-Pierre Valentine's wormhole.

"Sir, you have a visitor." His secretary announced.

"Ah, that was fast. Send them in."

"Faizan." A voice spoken softly said as a dark figure entered the office.

"How dare you address me in such a way!"

"Silence. You will listen to me." The visitor said. "You must not attempt to take the wormhole technology. You do not know what you are dealing with."

"That voice. It sounds so familiar." Faizan said.

"We have met."

"Who are you?"

"Someone you do not want to cross."

"Wait. I know that tone! Sims!"

Frank raised his head, to allow the light to touch his face. He smiled as he continued to speak.

"Yes. It is I. However, my name is not Sims. Now, heed my warning. It will be my last."

Frank closed his eyes and vanished just as quickly as before. Faizan became furious, shouting profanities as he called for his assistant.

"You called sir?" The assistant asked as he entered the office.

"No. I was just shouting your name for the fun of it! You are about as worthless as the others. I want all the information you can find on Lieutenant Sims."

That was definitely Centaurian technology. It is clear now, he is one of them.

"This cannot be good." Faizan said in a muffled tone.

The Centaurians were one of the alien races that the former United States government had been experimenting with them and their technology. Faizan knew if this was indeed a Centaurian that things were about to become difficult. They were known for being a race of peace and wanted to prevent wars.

"Sir, I have that information for you." The assistant stated as he entered.

"What did you find out?"

"He has been a member of the special forces for a while, he specializes in alien technology and reverse engineering. According to my additional research though, he is not from here."

"Explain. I know we discussed evidence of him possibly being from the Alpha Centauri system."

"There have been no reports of ships in our system for years. However, it appears we detected another wormhole event back around 2045."

"Why was I not informed of this?"

"I am not sure, it was before the unification process. Perhaps it was lost in the records. It was a faint reading, but there was most definitely a wormhole detected. It is possible that the Centaurians are traveling by wormhole now."

"That's how he did it." Faizan said.

He clinched his fist, pounding his desk.

"Sir?"

"Valentine. He could not have created a wormhole alone. He had access to alien technology."

"Sir, there is one other thing. I have intelligence reports that has him listed as a *Frank Valentine*."

"Wait. That would mean he is human. So which is it? Is he from the Alpha Centauri system or is he human?"

"Both sir."

"Both? Are you saying that there are humans living in space?"

"I am not sure how to explain it sir, but his medical records are accurate and he is human. However --" The assistant paused.

"However? What is it? Come on boy! I don't have all day."

"His DNA sir. It is very pure. No contaminates. Also, he has an implant."

"He has an implant? Then we should have access to it."

"No sir, it is not in our system. It is also a much more advanced implant and it appears to be linked into his entire neuromuscular system."

Faizan sat slowly into his chair, fists clinched. His brow was furrowed in concentration. He knew that only one thing could explain this. Frank was not Centaurian, but he had been in contact with them. This would be an issue and he knew things would get even more difficult with this revelation.

"Get him back! But don't let on that we know who he really is. I want to see his face when we deactivate his implant."

Faizan laughed, as he thought about his plan. If he could gain access to this implant, he could conquer two worlds.

♦

Frank arrived in Egypt where he would obtain the item he knew would help his grandparents on their new mission. What he wasn't expecting was the damage from the wars. So many of the pyramids had been severely damaged. He could sense the artifact nearby, but not in the original location.

"I know it is here, I can sense it." He thought aloud.

He had been taught about this artifact by Minister Gizelle and how it could be used to help humanity. A piece of technology that was left behind when the pyramids were built. Gizelle called it the *Beacon*. When activated, it would reveal the history of the Centaurians and how they had interacted with humanity from the beginning of time.

Frank approached the remains of the Great Pyramid of Giza. He could sense the artifact, but it was no longer there. It had been moved. He looked around, searching for anywhere that it could possibly be. If it was in the hands of the government there would be issues.

A young woman approached.

"Hello, my name is Mariam, welcome. I do not mean to pry, it is only that you appeared to be lost."

"I was just admiring the view. It is so sad to see the destruction to these amazing pyramids."

"Ah yes, you are a historian?" She asked.

"You could say that. And you?"

"Yes, I am a historian specializing in the great pyramids."

"May I ask, what happened to all of the artifacts?"

"Many of them are on display in the museum. Are you seeking a specific piece that you would like to see?"

"Actually, I am --" Frank paused.

He could sense something about Mariam. He closed his eyes, about to transport away when – he gasped. "You are Centaurian. I can sense it."

"I too can sense something within you. Please explain."

"My name is Frank Valentine."

"I do not recognize that name."

"This may be hard to explain. I am from Centaur."

"Impossible, you are human."

"Indeed. However, it is fact. I was born on the planet Centaur in the earth year of 2325. I was taught by the greatest, including my mentor Minister Gizelle Oorurah."

"Why are you here at this time?"

"This also may be hard to explain. As you are aware, this world has faced turmoil with wars and now a man set out to gain world domination, if not more. There were some changes that brought or will bring more chaos and the ultimate end to humanity before their time. My parents along with several others fled this planet to find safety and to rebuild the human race, in order to one day save the earth, sadly many died. Including many Centaurians."

"That is what I have been sensing. I felt there was something wrong."

"Yes. I was sent back to repair the time-lines, to the best of my abilities. Now I am seeking an artifact. Something --"

Mariam interrupted him. "I am the guardian of the *Beacon*. I can lead you to it. Be forewarned, it is a powerful device."

"I am uncertain as to why I was told about this. Before I left, Minister Gizelle told me of the *Beacon*, that if all else failed, this would be the guiding light for humanity."

"Indeed it can be. It can also become the final destruction if it it falls into the wrong hands. Faizan must never gain access to it. In his hands, he could destroy this entire planet. May I ask what you intend to use it for?"

"I was hoping you could tell me."

"The *Beacon* is a powerful source of energy. Properly used, it could power this entire world for a very long time. However, if someone like Faizan discovered the true power, it could --"

"Destroy the entire world." Frank finished her sentence.

"Yes. That is why this device has been hidden all of these years. When our people came to this world, we were hoping to offer peace. We helped to build these great pyramids, they would be a great source of energy. Sadly, the human race at that time was more interested in power and control, they began to worship our people as gods and that is not what we are."

"So, basically the world hasn't changed very much. Much of humanity is still more interested in power and control. The only exception is, they have turned from believing in any higher powers."

"This is true." Mariam said, feeling somewhat melancholy.

"How, may I ask, can this device help?" Frank asked.

"As you are aware, the world is in chaos. The energy sources were greatly diminished after the war. This device could restore the world and give unlimited energy to everyone."

Frank was silent, as he contemplated how this could help. He was to get a device that would give proof of things better. But how could this work? An alien technology would surely make things worse.

"I am unsure as to how this could help." Frank said. "It seems to me, this could bring forth confusion and lead to those such as Faizan wanting to have full control of it."

"You are correct. However, there is more to this device. It can do more than just provide energy. In fact, it is a source of power and knowledge. It contains vital records of historical significance. Including that of the creation."

"So you are saying this device contains evidence of creation?"

"Much more. The fact is, this device was never meant to fall into the hands of humanity. It was a record keeping device that the Centaurian people left behind to gather knowledge of the human race for future references, in the hopes that one day the people of earth would return to their roots of creation and faith."

"It sounds as if it is a library of some type." Frank said, as he thought for a moment on how this information could be of use.

"That and more. It is a very powerful device that can provide unlimited energy and history. Used properly, the *Beacon* can be a source to lead humanity in the right path."

"Revealing that knowledge at once could also be detrimental to the world, so this will need to be handled carefully."

"That is why I was assigned as the guardian, disguising myself as a historian so that I could have full access to the archives. You should understand, there are more artifacts that are hidden from humanity."

"Do you have them all?"

"I have access to them. Some are hidden in plain site, while others are protected in a high-level secured location that only I have access to."

"Indeed," Frank said with a raised brow. "How easily can these be accessed or *moved* if need be?"

"Moved? Why would I need to move them?"

"I have someone who will be a key to restoring the world."

Frank continued to inform Mariam of the recent events, how he became involved and the importance of his mission to save humanity. They discussed his grandparents and how they were now a vital part of the mission.

"Wow," Mariam said, "I cannot believe that you have been working so closely with your grandparents."

"Yes, and I feel that you are now a vital part of this mission also."

"If you have been taught by the Centaurians, then you know that we are not permitted to intervene."

"I understand, this is different though. You will be guiding the Valentines in their mission. The fact is, I do not believe Minister Gizelle would have led me to this device and apparently you, if he did not know that things could change and would require more."

"The fact that Faizan gained so much power so quickly leads me to think he has access to alien technology." Mariam said.

"That is a guarantee. The former United States was working with alien tech all along, reverse engineering it. They were not the only ones, just about all of the world's governments were."

"In that case, I have an idea."

"I'm open for suggestions. But, in the meantime, I suggest we find somewhere more private to talk, after all, I am a wanted man. I am sure Faizan has the entire One World government on the look out for me."

"This way, I have a place nearby."

She led Frank to a nearby building, it was a small store front that she used as a tourist office. Here she could maintain her cover as an Egyptian Historian all while protecting the *Beacon*.

"Nice cover job."

"It is more than a cover, it is my means of living while here on earth. I was given the greatest honor of being the guardian and I plan to uphold that position to the best of my abilities."

"I would expect no more from the guardian. I would expect no more than this from any Centaurian." Frank said as he joined his new friend at a small table.

They talked for a few minutes, as she told Frank all that she knew of the *Beacon* and other artifacts. Then she began to share her thoughts on how she could help.

"As I was saying, it is apparent that Faizan has access to tech beyond that of human design. I have sensed for a while now a presence beyond humanity. When you arrived, I though it was you."

"It is not me though. You are sensing the same sensation as I am."

"Another being of power, and I fear it is --" She paused.

"You know don't you? You know who they are."

"They have been known by humans as the Reptilians. Also as the Draconians."

"I remember lessons about them in my earth history and in my universal history classes on Centaur. They are a nasty group of conquerors. They chose to avoid earth at the time because they considered the human species to be too weak."

"But now --" Mariam paused and reached for a book.

She opened the book to a section that had been carved out. Hidden inside was a small computer tablet, similar to an iPad from the early twenty first century.

"Now, the human race has grown and they have returned. That is who we are both sensing." Frank said.

"Yes, I believe it is. Look here." She turned the screen where Frank could see, showing him a readout.

"What am I looking at?"

"This indicates any and all alien technology in operation on earth or nearby emitting an energy source. These indicators are showing a ship in high orbit. It is a Dragonoid vessel."

"Yes, I was taught that they were known as Dragonoids. Humans who had witnessed them, and survived, described them as a scaly humanoid with reptilian features." Frank said.

"Hence them being called Reptilians or Draconians. They are from a distant galaxy, with faster than light technology. Their home world is known as Dragonia. They quickly picked up on the human languages, as did the Centaurians. Due to their speech those who survived and heard them speak thought they said their home world was Draconia with a 'C'."

"From what I recall, they are a very nasty group. I suppose you do not have access to a weapon that could protect earth?"

"You know how we feel about violence. However, I do have access to alien technology besides that of Centaurian design."

"I take that as a yes," Frank said. "You said you had an idea?"

"We need to get the Dragonoids to reveal themselves. Then we need to make sure the world sees them and that they are helping Faizan."

"Can we get this tech to my grandparents' island?"

"I am able to teleport just as you. You need to access your bio-chip. Access teleport controls and increase the power by 35%, that should give us enough with mine together."

"We can transport ourselves and the tech at the same time."

Frank accessed his chip and did as she instructed. Mariam did the same and gathered a large crate from a hidden room inside her tourist office. They stood on either side of the crate, joined hands and then – a bright light plume appeared.

Chapter Sixteen

Operation Earth Defense

Valentine Island, Earth, 2105

Jean-Pierre sat with his wife, as they sipped on a tall glass of tea and enjoyed a sandwich. It had been several hours since Frank left.

"I hope Frank is safe." Sara said.

"I'm sure he is. He is Robert's son after all."

"He does have his *and your* intelligence."

"Sara, did we do the right thing?"

"Yes dear, I believe we did."

Sara sat quietly, her mind wondering. *I really miss my Robert.*

"You know Sara, I really see a lot of Robert in Frank. We can be so proud of our family."

"I agree," Sara said. "I do miss our son though. A lot."

"As do I my love, as do --"

A bright light filled the room as Frank appeared, with him, a new individual and a large crate. Jean-Pierre and Sara both were startled at the sudden appearance. They hadn't expected his return so soon and not with someone else.

"Frank! How dare you bring someone here!"

"Grandfather, please, let me explain --"

"Explain?" Jean-Pierre interrupted. "You brought a stranger to our island, putting your grandmother and I at risk."

"Dr. Valentine, please. My name is Mariam. I am Centaurian."

"Centaurian?" Sara questioned.

"Yes ma'am, I am a Centaurian. I have been here on earth as a guardian of the *Beacon* as well as other artifacts of extraterrestrial design."

"A guardian?" Jean-Pierre asked. "Why would the Centaurians have a guardian in place rather than just removing the technology from earth?"

"I wish I knew sir. All I know; I have instructions to protect the *Beacon* and the other artifacts until such time as they are needed to protect earth."

"Wait," Frank said. "You did not mention that part."

"You did not ask. I stated that I was the guardian of alien tech and that I had access to more than Centaurian tech. You asked if I had access to a weapon, did you not?"

"Yes."

"My reply was, I have access to alien technology besides that of Centaurian design. As you know, we are a non-violent race. It is apparent you are here for a purpose, as a human you apparently possess the human ability to fight."

"I do and I will."

"In that case," Mariam continued, "I will not stand in your way and I understand the circumstances. Therefore, I will provide you with a defense system. But first, we need to prepare a few things to give humanity a *Beacon* of hope."

She opened the crate and revealed a pyramid shaped object. It shone brightly with a golden gleam. The device had a base of about a half square meter and stood about one meter high.

"That reminds me of an Egyptian capstone." Jean-Pierre said as he examined the artifact.

"It should," Mariam said. "Because it is."

"How could it be?" Sara asked. "It is so small."

"This is the size it becomes for transport. When it is activated, it is much larger. It is hard to explain, in fact, I am not sure of all of the aspects of the device, other than how to activate it."

"There is much more to tell you grandfather." Frank said.

He told them about the Dragonoids and how they were the ones controlling Faizan. Jean-Pierre had already suspected there may be alien influence, but had kept this to himself.

Mariam explained how the device would work. It would generate enough power to get the attention of the Dragonoids. This would allow them to make their move to expose Faizan to the world. However, they had to be ready to stop them. This also meant revealing the *Beacon* and the Centaurians to the world.

"Frank, we need to talk, in private." Mariam said.

"Is something wrong?" Sara asked.

"No ma'am, I just need to talk to Frank about his role in this and to make sure we are on the same level."

Outside, Mariam began to explain how things would work and to give him more details on the available technology that could help, without the need for violence.

"I do not understand. If the Dragonoids are as powerful and dangerous as you describe, then as much as I hate to admit this, it may come to violence."

"You are correct in your understanding Frank, however, there is another way."

"I know we have the *Beacon*, but it is only an energy source, what other way could you have access to?"

"Luna." Mariam said.

"Luna? Who is she, another Centaurian?" Frank asked, clearly confused as to how someone else could be the answer.

"Not a person. A location. I am referring to the earth's moon, also know as Luna."

"I do not understand. How can a moon help us?"

"There is more to Luna than anyone realizes, although it has for a long time been speculated," Mariam paused. "Perhaps we should go back in, we can discuss this more with your grandparents. I have a feeling they will understand."

Mariam briefly informed Jean-Pierre of their discussion and how she had a plan that involved the earth's moon, Luna. He was intrigued, as was Sara and Frank, as to how the moon could help.

"I find your plan interesting." Jean-Pierre said.

"How can the moon help us though?" Sara asked.

"Dr. Valentine, are you familiar with any of the theories about the moon?"

"Which ones? There are so many." Jean-Pierre answered.

"The hollow moon theory." She stated.

"Are you telling me the moon really is hollow and is a space craft?

"No sir, not exactly. It is hollow, but it is not a ship. Let me see if I can explain."

She began to give a brief history of the moon and the creation period. She told of how the moon was a hollow shell, a very thick shell, but containing a hollow center. The Centaurians discovered this during the fall of the Roman Empire around the fifth century A.D., it was during this time, the Dragonoids made some of their first appearances on earth. The Centaurians knew they were a dangerous race and created a way to protect earth without the use of violence.

"Humans were on a path to learning more, with Christianity growing. Our people knew we had to protect humanity to allow them to grow. So, the moon became a base with an energy device that could stop the invasion without violence."

"How does this device work?" Frank asked.

"It is a device that produces an astronomical amount of power, power that can be used to open portals."

"How can this help us now?"

"That is where you and I come in. Frank, you possess part of the ability to activate this device."

Frank was more confused now than ever, with the timelines resetting, he was just beginning to regain full control of his bio-tech. Now he was being tasked to control some lunar weapon. How? That was his question. How could he possess the power or ability to achieve this?

"How will I activate this weapon?" Frank asked.

"It is not a weapon Frank. It is a very powerful energy source. As I said, it allows access to creating a massive portal, a one way portal."

"And this can help us how?" Jean-Pierre asked.

"Good question doctor. Let me see if I can answer this for you. As I stated, with the hollow center of the moon, this device was created to stop the invasion. A massive Centaurian base was installed inside the moon. The moon itself was then made into one large energy source, absorbing solar energy to power the base, this allowed the base to operate in secret all of these years."

"Wait, it is still an active base?" Sara asked.

"Not entirely. After the invasion was stopped, the base became inactive and the caretakers were placed into long term stasis units. Until such time they were needed again."

"So, all of these years --" Jean-Pierre paused.

"The moon has been an inactive or dormant base." Frank said.

"Yes, and now Frank, you are here and humanity is facing another invasion. You and I can save them, but we only have one shot at this."

"Does this mean we have to go to the moon?" Frank asked.

"No. Our job will be to work from here. And your grandfather will have a major role in this also, using the *Beacon*. I need you to access your implant, search for a file titled Luna Omega, I am sure you will have it. Once you access it, enter the code word; Omega. This will awaken the caretakers and then I can communicate with them."

"Accessing the file now."

Frank closed his eyes as he accessed the file and entered the code word. He could sense a great power as the base began to activate. Mariam was also sensing this. She began to focus on the caretakers, knowing that they would be seeking out a guardian who would instruct them on their mission.

"The systems are coming online now. We must be careful, we only want to awaken the caretakers, not alert the Dragonoids to what we are doing." Mariam said.

"It is done. Systems are online." Frank said as he opened his eyes to see Mariam now focused on her role as the guardian.

"What is happening now?" Jean-Pierre asked.

"She is focusing on the caretakers as they come out of stasis, they will be seeking out the guardian. The only reason they would be awakened is if humanity is facing extreme danger, so they will be seeking guidance as to their next move."

"So you are saying that we are about to engage in some sort of space war?" Sara asked, nervously.

"No, not if we can help it. Mariam will give them instructions on how to proceed. Their main role is to protect humanity. As you know, the Centaurians are a peaceful people, they will avoid violence at all cost. Our goal is to activate this device, which will open a portal to essentially teleport the Dragonoids back to their galaxy."

"What happens when they return again?" Jean-Pierre asked.

"We will discuss that when this is taken care of. Let's go talk over here, where she can concentrate."

Frank and Jean-Pierre talked more as they made their way to the other side of the room. This would give their new friend the time she needed to communicate with the caretakers. Frank tried to explain the full mission to his grandfather. He was still unsure of everything, but Jean-Pierre was starting to understand more.

"Gentlemen, the caretakers have been briefed. They are now waiting on the next move. Dr. Valentine, that next move will be on the part of you and your wife."

"Wait, I don't understand," Sara said. "What can we do?"

"Grandfather, you have access to satellites that can allow you to send a message to the entire world at once. We plan to use that to our advantage."

"In order to broadcast a message on that scale, I would need access to the One World Earth networks. As of now, I do not have that access."

"But I do. I can access the systems myself with the help of my implant." Frank said.

"You plan to hack into the O.W.E. Satellites?" Sara asked.

"Yes. That is the only way to gain access and to allow you the tools to create and broadcast our message. We will also, at the same time, prepare to broadcast live video feed of the Dragonoid ship in orbit."

"You plan to tip the hand in our favor." Jean-Pierre said.

"Yes, but we want the public to realize that Faizan is under the influence of an evil alien species." Frank said.

"The problem is," Mariam said. "We have to also convince the public that we are here to help. Humanity has a hard time dealing with change or with extraterrestrial beings."

"There is so much at stake here grandfather, and I know it is a hard time with the world right now. We have the caretakers on standby. There is one problem, I am still uncertain if this is what my mission was meant to be."

"Frank, you need to access all of your implant files. If there is a directive for your mission embedded into your programming you should be able to access it." Mariam said.

"Perhaps I should meditate and pray."

"That is a good idea. I know you have been taught well."

"Pray? Here we go again, humanity is literally on the brink of destruction and he wants to *pray.*"

"Jean-Pierre, now is not the time for your agnostic judgments. We have already seen the results of his praying, including you. You have seen the results and you know it." Sara said.

"Fine. I suppose we need it now more than an ever. If there really is a higher power here, then we need all the help we can possibly get."

"Dr. Valentine, sir, please trust your grandson and please have faith in the Creator."

"Mariam, can we talk, in private?" Sara motioned for their new friend to join her in the kitchen.

"I asked you in here, that we might speak more freely. As I am sure you can tell, my husband has a hard time with religion."

"This seems to be an issue with humanity as a whole, lately."

"Yes, as sad as that is, it is the truth. People have turned their backs on God."

"Not everyone," Mariam said. "I can sense a great deal of faith within your spirit."

"Is it true that your people witnessed creation?"

"Not to say we were here when it happened. However, we witnessed the creation of this universe from our home realm. We come from a dimension that parallels this one. When we saw that the Creator had created such a beautiful universe, many of our people chose to visit and make it our home. We wanted to see what it would become."

"Not so beautiful now is it?"

"On the contrary, it is his creation and everything he creates is beautiful."

"I feel the same way. But, I have to ask you, where did the Dragonoids come from?"

"They too came from another dimension."

"If God created everything, why would he allow such a race to exist?"

"The same reason he allows humanity to continue. Although, he has chosen on more than one occasion to destroy everything and start over. However, after he chose to become human by allowing his spirit to beget a child, called Immanuel – a name later rendered Emmanuel in the New Testament—things changed. Now, it is up to humanity to choose the right path."

"You know so much about the bible. I assume you have studied the scriptures a great deal during your time here."

"I have, however, it is part of our teachings on Centaur as well, since we have chosen to be the guardians of this world. We have seen the potential that humanity has and we know that they will make the right choices."

"Please don't misjudge Jean-Pierre, he is a good man."

"Oh no my dear, I would never do that. I can sense in his spirit as well that he believes, albeit he is fighting with doubt."

"Yes, he has for so many years questioned the existence of God and creation. Now, with all that is happening, his life that revolved around science has been turned upside down."

"The Creator has a way of doing that sometimes to get the attention of his creation."

Sara smiled at these words of comfort and wisdom coming from their new friend. Just as she was about to say something, she heard Frank calling for them to come.

"We have a little issue." Frank said as the women joined he and his grandfather.

"What is it?" Mariam asked.

"As stated, in order to achieve this, we will need to convince the world that Faizan is under the influence of alien tech. That may present a problem."

"I don't understand, I thought this was already worked out as to how we would do this." Sara said.

"We have, but we have a new issue. And it is me."

"You?" Mariam questioned.

"Yes. I am having trouble accessing the files, there seems to be a block in place that requires a code that only I can know."

"So what is the issue?" Jean-Pierre asked.

"I cannot remember it. Until I met Mariam, I had forgotten that I could access so many files and programming modes."

"Perhaps," Sara began, "the time-lines have not fully reset."

"This is possible," Mariam said. "Since the time-lines have went through a reset, of sorts, it is possible that your time-line is still moving forward to the point you return."

"Which means I may not have been given the code yet."

"Or you could not get it at all." Sara said.

"What happens then?" Jean-Pierre asked.

"That is something we will have to work around. But at this time, I say we take it slow. The Dragonoids will not make a move this early into everything. So, we lay low for now." Mariam said.

"Things have changed in my mission," Frank said. "That is a fact I cannot avoid. It was apparent my original mission was to save lives, including my grandparents. That was accomplished and time-lines were affected. Now we have the Dragonoids and I am not sure what my mission is now. I am having new memories and things I knew, or thought I knew, I no longer know."

◆

Frank chose to meditate a while, hoping that something would come to him. Perhaps he would see something in his spirit that would trigger a memory. Perhaps he would remember a way that all of this would not happen.

There was a great deal of work to be done. Jean-Pierre worked to prepare the camera equipment while Sara and Mariam talked more about historical events.

"This is one of the issues with time travel, when you make changes in the time-lines, it can affect the traveler, including their memory. Perhaps meditation will help him to gain some of those new memories." Sara Said.

"You and your husband are well versed in the sciences."

"We have worked in this field for many years, that is how we met."

"Sara, you are a faithful believer, someone who truly believes. Has your husband always had so much doubt?"

"No. At one time, he too was a firm believer – then, it happened. That day in the lab, when that first particle appeared. It is as if all of his belief was shattered."

"Sadly, that is how those spirits of doubt work. The enemy of the Creator, you call him Satan, uses things like doubt. When he sees an opportunity, he will go for it."

"I have found myself feeling a little doubt, with the discovery of alien-beings and technology. But, I know there is more than I realize, that God has a plan."

"I understand Sara, I suggest you pray, we will talk later. I need to meditate a little myself."

♦

After a brief meditation, Mariam took time to give a little history lesson on all of the artifacts she had that were actually alien technology. This of course had all of Jean-Pierre's attention. He was very interested in how the *Beacon* worked and what the main purpose was for it. They spent what seemed to be hours discussing everything Mariam knew.

Sara of course was preoccupied with her thoughts, wondering how Robert was doing and worried about Frank and how this was affecting him. It had to be hard, so far from the home he knew. She watched as he sat under the stars that were now brightly shining in the evening sky. His mind was so strong, yet it was missing so many new or *renewed* memories. She could see her grandson staring off into the stars, in deep thought, meditating and she was sure, praying.

Something has to come to him. She thought.

"Mariam, I am sorry to interrupt your history lesson, but what happens if Frank can't regain access to the files?" Sara asked.

"That is something we will have to face if the need arises, however, I feel that with a little more time he will access those files. The only concern we have is whether or not the changes in the time-lines have affected his bio-chip."

Sara looked out at her grandson again. He had been in deep meditation and prayer for hours, she was sure he was tired but she was also sure that he would find the answers he sought.

Chapter Seventeen
A New Mission

Centaur Ministry of Science, 2345

"Frank, your mother and I are so proud of the man you have become. This mission is very dangerous, I know you will do well and make a difference in humanity." Robert said as he prepared his son for his mission.

"I know what I must do. I must continue the original mission that you started so long ago."

"Frank, I am happy to see you. We have something to discuss. If you and your father would join me. The Ministry of Science has developed a few updates for your implant." Minister Gizelle said as he approached the Valentines.

The three made their way to meet with the Ministry of Science. In route, Minister Gizelle gave more instructions in regards to the mission. Although the Centaurians have used their technology for distant travels, as well as time travel, this mission had significance. There was so much at stake, not just for humanity, but for all of creation.

"We are here," Gizelle said. "Perhaps you should wait here. I will let the ministry know you are ready."

The father and son duo waited just outside as Minister Gizelle announced their presence. Since arriving on Centaur, many things had changed. The fleet was now in full operation with Robert now holding a rank of Admiral, per the the Council of Centaur. Frank was about to embark on a mission to save humanity from an unknown source. All that had been revealed to him about this source was that the council could sense a major disruption in the time-line from earth around the year 2105, which was when the fleet left for the wormhole. There was still so much that was not known, not even to the Centaurians. It would be up to Frank to correct anything.

"Admiral, it appears this meeting is very sensitive, they have asked to see Frank alone." Gizelle said as he returned.

"Understood."

"Frank, you go ahead in, your father and I need to talk about a few things here."

"Yes minister. Thank you."

Frank made his way into the council chambers to meet with the Ministry of Science. He was about to learn more in regards to his mission.

"Good day Frank, please have a seat." A tall, blonde female member of the Ministry of Science motioned to a single chair in the middle of the room.

"Thank you minister. I am pleased to be here."

"My name is Ophelia, I trust your day has been well. I know we do not get around to meeting everyone, as we are continually monitoring the galaxy for any threats to our world, or earth. Sadly Frank, that day has come in regards to the aforementioned threat."

"I will do what I need in order to protect our people minister."

"I am sure of that. You are a special young man. I cannot tell you much about the threat, as it appears to happen on a different plane of time. I can tell this however, we sense a very powerful entity."

"What do you request of me?"

Ophelia conversed with the other council members in their native language, of which Frank was quickly learning; however, he was unfamiliar with this dialect.

"Frank Jean-Pierre Valentine, please stand." Instructed a male figure who spoke with a deep, powerful tone.

Frank stood, not speaking a word. Though he was a stout man, he was feeling a little anxious with the council member's tone.

"Frank, as you are now aware," Ophelia began. "Humanity and the galaxy is facing a powerful and dangerous threat. You are also aware that the Centaurians are peaceful."

"Yes minister. I am aware of this."

"You are also aware that because of this, we cannot defend our world. We would rather die than to take another life. No matter the reason."

"Minister Ophelia, I apologize if I am out of line. I understand the history of the Centaurian people, I also respect your stance on violence. I too would rather choose peace over violence."

"I am not sure you are understanding this mission."

Frank thought for a moment as to why they would want him, why they would choose a human with the abilities that he has for this mission.

"I think I understand the mission. I am the only answer, since I possess the human emotions. You know, that if the need arises I can and will fight."

"We hope, young Valentine," Minister Gizelle said as he entered the chambers. "That it does not come to that."

"Minister Oorurah, please, join us." Ophelia said, with a bow of her head to their leader.

"Frank, your mission will be dangerous, but there are some things we will provide that will help, when the time comes. Our scientist have worked to develop new programming for your biochip." Gizelle said.

"New programming?" Frank questioned.

"I will explain it all when we get back to your home. I would like to have the admiral with us when we discuss this. He will meet us there, along with your mother."

The science council adjourned the meeting, escorting Frank to the lab. There he would undergo the upgrades to his implant. He was still feeling somewhat anxious; Minister Gizelle sensed this anxiety and assured Frank that all would be well.

"Frank, just relax. You have been through upgrades before, this is no different." Gizelle said.

"I know, but I sense something – danger."

The science council began the upgrades, which took a very short time to complete. Frank would have new files he could access in time of need.

"I feel no change." Frank said.

"We will discuss it all when we get to your home. There are so many things we need to talk about, some that even I nor the others can fully sense."

Frank had never seen his mentor like this. He could sense a great fear, which was one of the only other emotions, besides love and sadness, he had ever sensed from the Centaurians. They met with Robert outside the chambers where they made their way back to their home. Frank was quiet in route, as he tried to understand the upgrades he had just underwent.

◆

"Frank. Frank, are you listening to me?" Robert asked as they stood outside their home. Frank was in deep thought as he tried to understand everything.

"Oh sorry, I was just thinking."

"I can see that, the minister and I were just talking about your upgrades. He was explaining a few things and you just zoned out. Are you okay?"

"Yes. I am sorry Minister Gizelle."

"It is fine my young friend. You have a lot on your mind, and rightly so. I was just telling your father about your upgrades."

"I have been trying to understand what it is they did. I feel no changes."

"As I was telling your father, your upgrades will include a number of hidden files, accessible only by a code word. Prior to your mission, those code words will be uploaded into your chip. They will become accessible, only when you need them most."

"How will I access them?"

"You will have files that will be dormant, those files will contain the codes needed. They will activate automatically, as the need arises." Gizelle stated as they sat around the table sipping tea.

"I am not sure I like this." Jill said.

"Mom, it will be okay."

"How will those files activate?" Robert asked.

"Through a sequence of events. I am not sure I can explain it properly for you. As Frank proceeds with his mission, the time-lines will go through changes. As those changes progress, files will begin to activate. However, Frank, we will embed selective thoughts or phrases that will help those files to become active. At that point, you will gain access to the code words required."

"Phrases?" Frank asked. "What phrases? Am I supposed to hear a certain phrase that will enable me to access the code word or will it be a phrase I know already?"

"As the time-lines change," Gizelle began, "you will – undergo memory lapses as well as regaining certain memories. The best way to explain this would be that you will know when the time comes. There are ways to help your memories to surface, through meditation. I suggest you meditate as often as you can."

"Understood."

"Gentlemen, I must retire for the evening in preparation for the mission."

After Minister Gizelle left, Frank and his parents spent their evening talking, knowing that this could be the last time they see one another.

"Are you worried son?" Jill asked.

"Not really, I mean – maybe a little."

"Son, it is a wise man who faces the unknown with at least a little fear, as it helps him to stay focused and alert. A foolish man faces the unknown without fear, for without it, he would not be alert to any dangers." Robert said.

"But did not the bible teach that we should not fear? So, why should I fear?" Frank asked.

"Yes my son," Jill said. "However, we must understand that God was teaching us not to bow to fear, rather to understand that He is with us in all that we face."

"I think I understand mom."

The Valentines went to bed, as they would need to get an early start for the mission. Meanwhile, Minister Gizelle met with the other council members to prepare all that was needed. Including one additional piece of information he would need to access the files. A sense of danger continued to fill the air, the council members all could sense this. They knew the time was now, the galaxy was in danger, Frank was their hope to correct this. The time had come.

"Good morning Admiral, Vice Admiral. I assume Frank has rested well." Minister Gizelle said, arriving to escort the family to the mission site.

"I did." Frank said as he entered the room. "I assume we are ready to proceed?"

"Indeed. You appear to be ready to go."

"I am."

It was a slow journey to the mission site, as the Valentines took time together, perhaps for the last time. Minister Gizelle did not rush them, as he could sense the intensity of the moment.

"We have arrived." Gizelle said. "Frank, before we begin, we need to provide you with an additional piece of information."

"What is it?"

"A simple phrase. This phrase will enable you to access files as it becomes necessary."

Frank gave his parents one last hug before beginning his mission. The council members had activated the special phrase into his bio-chip. When the time came, it would activate his memory files. The mission was now ready to begin. Frank chose to meditate one more time, prior to leaving, remembering the things his mentor had told him on their way to the site.

♦

"Jill, don't worry, Frank will be fine."

"I know, after all, he is your son and he is just like you. Strong willed and intelligent."

The Valentines watched as their son vanished in a plume of light, knowing this could very well be the last time they ever see him. The mission site was silent.

"Admiral," Gizelle broke the silence as he approached. "Your son will do well. I can sense that he has arrived. Now, we wait, we watch and we pray."

"How will we know if the mission is a success?" Jill asked.

Minister Gizelle was silent, as he considered the answer to the Vice-Admiral's question.

"We can be certain of one thing. You are here, we are at this moment in time. That is a good sign. Understand this, certain things have already been put into motion. Certain events have taken place that will or have already led to this point in time."

"I am not sure I understand." Robert said.

"Time travel is hard to comprehend." Jill added.

"Indeed my friends. Let me see if I can explain. We have already witnessed events take place. The fact that you are here. The attack on our people. Those events took place, because of this moment in time."

"Now I am really confused." Robert said.

"When we first met, if you recall, there was something about the time-lines that was – off. We knew that there was something that would take place in the future, that would lead to the events that had taken place. We also knew that we had to step in to correct those events."

"So you are saying that Frank is the reason behind the attacks, the sabotage and everything else that has happened?"

"Admiral, there are many things that brought on these events. The experiments that your father started, they were the key factor to everything. We had to send someone back in time to stop a chain of events from taking place that would lead to the destruction of life on earth. Your father saw something that day."

"I remember a story he told, of a figure he saw in the light. At the time, he thought it was an illusion. Mom and I always wondered what he really saw. Are you saying it was Frank?"

"Yes and no. Time travel, as I stated, is hard to comprehend."

Jill stood quietly, thinking about the things she had just heard.

"I think I understand, before we left, Robert's mother and I did some theoretical studies in regards to time travel. Although Frank may not be the cause of the events, his presence will play a crucial role in the events as they happen."

"Indeed. That is correct, at this point, we will have to wait as the events unfold. What we have experienced has happened. That is a fact, but there are still things in motion, things that only Frank can control. Those events have yet to take place, at least not in the current realm of reality. Many things can and will take place in his mission. We do not know of those things, however, I am sure when --" Gizelle paused, considering what he should say at that point. "When he returns, I am sure he will tell us what happened."

Robert could detect the concern in Gizelle's voice, but he trusted him.

Chapter Eighteen
Operation Earth Defense
Valentine Island, Earth, 2105

Frank was meditating in the clearing while the others waited patiently inside.

"This is too much." Jean-Pierre said. "We are running out of time here and he is out there praying!"

"Please, be patient Doctor. Your grandson is doing what he needs to be doing in order to gain more access to the files we need. There has to be something there, *the directive file* that will allow access."

Just as Mariam stated this, Frank walked in.

"What did you just say?"

"There has to be something there."

"No, you mentioned a file, you called it *the directive file*."

Just then, Frank sensed a flood of new memories, allowing him to access more files.

"Frank, are you okay?" Sara asked.

No response.

"Frank?" Jean-Pierre tried to get his grandson's attention, touching his shoulder. "Frank, can you hear me?"

He stumbled slightly as he regained his thoughts.

"Frank?"

"I – I'm okay grandfather. I know the code word."

"Are you sure?" Mariam asked.

"Yes. It is time. We must prepare the *Beacon*."

"It is ready, all we need is the access code." Sara said.

Frank worked with Mariam to prepare the *Beacon*. Mariam also instructed the caretakers in their roles for the mission. Sara and Jean-Pierre worked to prepare their statement to the world, it would need to be flawless. Any mistakes now could prove to be detrimental to the mission.

"Is everyone ready?" Mariam asked.

"We are as ready as we can be." Frank said as they gathered in the field.

Jean-Pierre prepared a camera for their broadcast. It would be used to go live around the world with the help of the O.W.E. Satellite systems. The overall plan was to reveal to the world at one time the existence of extraterrestrial life and technology on earth. At the same time, they would reveal that Faizan was under the direct influence of alien-beings. This would come through the help of the caretakers who, somehow, had a way to reveal them, even if they are cloaked.

"Frank, once you access the files, we will transmit them to the caretakers. They will then know what steps to take. Doctor Valentine, you and your wife will begin your broadcast shortly after this. So you need to be ready to go."

"Understood." The three Valentines responded in unison.

"This will be the moment that can bring ultimate peace or – it could bring destruction if we are not careful. We need to prepare for the worst, while hoping for the best in this." Mariam said.

"But the caretakers can help us to fight them off, right?"

"No grandfather, the role of the caretakers is not to fight, they are here to guide. Remember, the Centaurian people are a people of peace."

"Your grandson is correct, however, in this case, the caretakers will provide the technology to send the enemy far away, in a non-violent way."

They continued to prepare everything for the broadcast. Sara worked closely with Mariam. Frank chose this time to meditate further, focusing on the files needed for their mission to succeed. Jean-Pierre carefully went over his speech, being careful to miss nothing of importance. He knew this was the only way to make the world see the truth.

"Doctor Valentine, we are ready here." Mariam announced.

"I am ready when you are." He replied.

"Sara, I need you to operate the camera. When we activate the *Beacon*, you will focus the camera on it. Showing the world the power as we switch everything over."

"How will we show the power?" Jean-Pierre asked.

"In your speech, you will announce that the world power grid is about to fall, at that time, the caretakers will cut the power all at once worldwide. Simultaneously, the *Beacon* will be activated, sending the power to the entire world, with more energy than anyone could imagine. You will explain, no, reassure the world that you have access to technology to provide unlimited energy to the world."

"One more thing," Frank added as he joined the others. "We must protect the faith of the people. We must not allow this to deter their faith in the Creator."

"Look, we don't have time for this." Jean-Pierre snapped.

"He is right Doctor Valentine. It is imperative that the Creator is recognized and the faith is maintained." Mariam said.

"They are right my love, we must do this."

"Fine. We'll do it your way." Jean-Pierre retorted as he finished the camera set-up.

"Frank," Sara said, "how will we acknowledge God for this? You know your grandfather is not the one to handle such."

"Once the *Beacon* has been activated, I will then introduce Mariam and we will tell how her people have been here since the dawn of creation. I know it will be hard for people to comprehend. At this time, Mariam will tell her story of how it all began." Frank said.

"That is an option," Mariam began, "however, I am not sure the people will listen to me. We must find a way to convince the world that faith is the only way to move forward."

Sara thought for a moment, reaching for her bible she turned to the scriptures.

"Faith is the substance of things hoped for." She read aloud as she began to read from the book of Hebrews.

"Grandmother?"

"We read from the scriptures, then we bring on Mariam."

"I like that idea." Mariam said.

Jean-Pierre scoffed at the idea. He was convinced this was a bad idea. He knew the people of this time period had left the way of faith based religions a long time ago. Yes, there were several who still believed, however, he felt that number was so minuscule that it didn't matter.

"That is absurd!" Jean-Pierre shouted. "A waste of time and a waste of energy. We need to just get to the point!"

"It is imperative that we include a message of faith. Without it this world as we know it will continue to fall to evil." Sara said.

"She is right," Frank said. "It is a must that we do this."

"Without faith, without hope, the world cannot change. We must give the people hope." Mariam said.

"So, this is the plan then. We will begin the broadcast, as planned. Before introducing Mariam, I will read from the bible, reassuring everyone that there is hope."

"I have a question for you all," Jean-Pierre began. "How are we going to convince the people that she is an alien-being?"

"I will take care of that. I will show them who I really am, let them see the real me." Mariam replied.

"You are going to reveal your true self to the world, your true appearance, aren't you?" Frank asked.

"Yes. It is the only way."

"Your true appearance?" Jean-Pierre questioned.

"Yes. This form you see before you is not how my people look in our true form. We take on this appearance to blend in."

Mariam began to explain that her people, the Centaurian race, did not look as she does. She described their true appearance.

"You just described what was known as the 'Grays' during the UFO movements of the twentieth and twenty first centuries. They were a race of tall, slender, alien-beings that fit your description perfectly." Jean-Pierre said.

"Yes, those sightings were true. However, many of the tales were exaggerated or completely false." Mariam responded.

Mariam continued to explain how she would reveal her true identity to the world, and she would do this live. As soon as the broadcast begins, the *Beacon* will be activated on queue. This would all be accomplished in steps. Jean-Pierre would begin the broadcast, informing the world that the entire power grid would fail. He would also share the message of hope, that he has access to technology that will provide great power to everyone. At that point, Frank will transmit the code to the Caretakers who will then cut the power, at the same time, the *Beacon* would activate. The power would be so intense that the *Beacon* would be seen from all over. This would then return power to the world.

The next step would be for Sara to focus the camera on the power source and then share the scriptures. Mariam explained that she would at that time, join her on camera, revealing her true identity live for everyone to see.

Jean-Pierre thought for a moment before interrupting. "We haven't thought of everything."

"What do you mean?" Frank asked.

"We need to convince the world that Faizan is under the influence of alien-beings all while we are convincing them to trust alien-beings." He responded.

"That is the point of the *Beacon*, that will help to prove to the world that..." Mariam was interrupted.

"You are not listening to me!" Jean-Pierre shouted.

Now frustrated, he stormed off to his lab, as the others stood in dismay as to what just happened.

"I'll go talk to him." Sara said.

Sara left to talk with her husband while Frank and Mariam discussed their options. Perhaps there was something to the doctor's concerns.

"Frank," Mariam began. "Your grandfather is set in his ways, however, he may have a point."

"What should we do, the plan is already in motion."

"I will contact the caretakers. We need to let them know what is happening."

Mariam focused her thoughts, focusing on the caretakers. She needed to convey the possible changes that was taking place. Frank chose this time to meditate, hoping there was something within his memory, perhaps a message given by his mentor.

Chapter Nineteen

Centaur Ministry of Science, 2345

Prior to Departure

Frank had been meditating frequently, knowing that his mission would be one of historic value. He wanted to prepare his mind, body and soul for this important mission. He knew things would be difficult, there would be a lot of things he would have to face. He knew his mission, he knew the time-lines would be affected. How much? He was unsure of. What if he failed? What if he made mistakes? There were so many things that could go wrong with this mission.

Minister Gizelle could sense the concerns within his spirit. He too knew there were certain risks. Although the Centaurians had a *connection* with the universe, allowing them to sense changes, he could not foresee everything. Sending someone, especially a human, back in time was a risk. The slightest change could prove catastrophic.

"Minister, you seem extra quiet." Robert said. "Is everything okay?"

"Yes, I am fine."

Robert knew better. There was definitely concern in the air. They could all sense that, no special connections to the universe were needed for that.

"Admiral, I know you are a wise man. Yes, I have been quiet. I know that sending Frank back in time is a great risk. We all know this."

"What are the chances – I mean, what if things go wrong?"

Robert was clearly concerned for his son's life. Not knowing what could await him back on earth.

"I cannot give you a definitive answer. We know there are risks involved in this mission."

161

"It is still a lot to think about. This is my son we are talking about."

"Let us allow Frank to meditate a little longer. It is now up to him."

Frank meditated for about an hour, before joining his mentor and his parents for a brief visit and family meal before his departure. He was feeling more secure in his mission, however, the concerns were valid. Time was of the essence, they would make this a short visit and then proceed with their plans.

"Frank, I want you to understand. This mission is entirely your choice." Gizelle said as they made their way to the mission site.

"I understand. I want to do this, I need to do this."

"I have asked the Ministry of Science to give you one more update to your implant. It will guide when the time comes. You will need to focus, when the need arises, all of your energy. Seek out the answers. What may seem logical at the time could very well lead to disaster and failure."

"Failure?" Robert and Jill asked in unison.

"Yes. But Frank is capable of this mission, the council trusts his abilities."

"I think I understand. It will be a difficult mission and I know, that with the Creator on my side, it will be a successful mission."

"Yes, always trust in the Creator, as he will guide you along the way. Also trust in your instincts as you will recognize when something needs more than you anticipate." Gizelle said.

The time had come, Frank was about to embark on a mission that would take him on a rare journey. He was about to face more than any human had ever faced before. He closed his eyes, focusing on the energy within him. A bright plume of light filled the area, as the energy grew into a portal, sending Frank back in time; back to the start of it all, of all that they were now facing. The light that had enveloped Frank, was now filling the entire area with auroras and energy like none had felt before. A bright testament of Frank's journey and what would lie ahead for him on this journey. His parents watched, as their son went forth on a mission to save humanity.

Chapter Twenty
No Turning Back Now
Valentine Island, Earth, 2105

"There is no turning back now, we have to move forward with this." Sara said.

"Agreed, we must see this through. I know that your husband has his doubts, but we must complete this mission. We must go forward." Mariam said as Frank joined them.

Frank had been talking with his grandfather, trying to convince him that this would work. However, Jean-Pierre had valid concerns with the plan and Frank was now concerned as well.

"Ladies, we need to talk."

"Frank? What is wrong?" Sara asked.

"I feel that grandfather has some valid concerns and I am now wondering if our plan will be successful. I do have another plan, a way that we can still do this."

"I am open to suggestions." Mariam said.

"We still use the networks to broadcast a message, but we need to expose Faizan immediately. Mariam, you will instruct the care-takers to reveal the Dragonoids once we go live. At the same time, we will move forward with the plan to give a message of hope and faith. We then introduce Mariam as she reveals her true form."

Frank continued to give details of his plan, a plan that included more or less the original plan. With a few minor changes. This would be a risk, one that could lead to the Dragonoids making their move ahead of time. It was a risk they had to take.

Jean-Pierre joined the others as they discussed the changes. He was still frustrated, but he knew this had to be done.

"Okay," Jean-Pierre began, "where are we at on this?"

Just then an alarm sounded, it was the One World Earth alert system, alerting the citizens of an important message.

"What now?" Sara asked, as she turned on a monitor.

◆

"Citizens of One World Earth. All hail Prime Minister Akeem Faizan!" A voice announced.

Mariam shivered at the appearance of the Prime Minister on the monitor. "He is pure evil." She said as she watched him standing there, a crowd shouting "Hail" with outstretched arms. A striking resemblance to the days of Nazi Germany that she had witnessed so many years ago as a young guardian.

Faizan began his announcement. "Great citizens of One World Earth, we have traitors among us!" He shouted this message, his eyes glaring with a darkness.

Just then, two men were brought onto the stage, both with their heads covered. As the hoods were removed, Jean-Pierre immediately recognized them as two of his friends. They also had rejected the new government.

"These two traitors have blatantly refused to follow our laws, to bring peace to this world. Therefore, they will be set forth as examples of what happens when you betray my leadership!"

Two guards then pulled out their guns, shooting both men for everyone to witness.

"Now, there are others out there, by the name of Valentine who have betrayed our ways." Faizan looked into the camera, as if he were staring directly at Jean-Pierre. "Doctor Valentine, I will give you and your wife one chance to turn yourselves in along with that traitor who is helping you."

◆

"What are we going to do now?" Sara asked.

"We proceed as planned." Jean-Pierre replied.

"I agree." Frank said. "We proceed as planned. Mariam, you will still instruct the caretakers to reveal the Dragonoids once we are live. At the same time we need to find a way to show Faizan as well."

"He always has cameras following him, broadcasting live. Can we use that as a way to reveal him at the same time? Would we be able to do that?" Sara asked.

"I think we can." Jean-Pierre replied. "I can do a simulcast."

"Mariam," Frank said, "we need to talk, in private."

She followed him to the clearing, where they would deploy the *Beacon*. There, Frank shared his thoughts and concerns with his friend.

"You stated that contained within the *Beacon* is a library of sorts and I think we can use that to our advantage."

"Yes, however, we must be careful in what we reveal. If we reveal too much at once, it could bring chaos."

"We have no choice. Let me ask this; can you choose what is revealed?"

"Of course. What do you have in mind?"

Frank thought long on this. He knew that there would need to be something of significance in order to convince everyone. What was that information? What did Minster Gizelle tell him before he left?

Think Frank, think. What did he tell me?

"I know what we need!" He shouted.

"What is it?" Mariam asked.

"You said that the *Beacon* contains all of earths history in the records. We need to find a specific time in history, something that everyone is aware of, but something that will spark their faith."

"I think I have just the event in mind." She responded.

Mariam prepared the *Beacon* for the broadcast. She instructed the others in what was needed. They would need to prepare an area of approximately 144 square feet. There could be nothing above. Once the *Beacon* activated, it would expand in size.

"I think we are about ready." Sara said as she and Mariam discussed the special message that would be given.

"I hope you know what you are doing." Jean-Pierre said.

"Grandfather, please, trust us."

"I just think we need to focus on exposing the aliens and what they are doing with Faizan. All of this religious nonsense is a waste of time in my opinion."

"Please my love, trust them. Frank and Mariam know what they are doing."

He scoffed at the notion, but ultimately agreed to it. In his heart, he knew what they were saying was true. Although he had doubted the existence of God for so long, he knew there was more to the universe. The discoveries he had made in his research indicated more, but the science community was set on denying this. To them, they held that a singular cosmic event took place, that led to the random development of bacteria which in turn grew and evolved into more complex life, leading to the evolution of human beings.

Jean-Pierre knew within his own heart there was more. In order to fit in with the others and to be considered trusted in his field of research, he chose to ignore his feelings. By doing this, he allowed doubt to take over what he knew to be the more logical and, though many disagree, the more scientific approach. After all, many scientist adamantly believe in the multiverse theory. So why couldn't there be some being with the power to create?

"If we are going to do this," Jean-Pierre began, "I feel we need to cover a few things. First, we need to get the attention of the world. Frank, can you also access the alert system?"

"I believe we can."

"What do you have in mind doctor?" Mariam asked.

"By sounding the alert system, this will cause everyone, or at least those who are able, to tune into the broadcast. They of course would be expecting Faizan. We will then begin our broadcast. I will share my thoughts on the multiverse. We can then proceed with the rest of the plan." Jean-Pierre said.

"I think I understand what you are planning," Sara said, joining the conversation. "We will gain their attention and then reveal all we have."

"Yes, this could work, but we must be quick, I am sensing something wrong." Mariam said.

"I too feel something." Frank added.

"Is it possible that Faizan knows something?" Sara asked.

"I am not sure, it has been a very long time since we last encountered the Dragonoids. It is possible they have become stronger, more advanced. If they are in some way detecting any alien technology outside of their own, they could be giving that information to Faizan." Mariam said.

"Mariam, perhaps you should communicate with the care-takers to see if they too sense anything." Frank suggested.

"Wait!" Jean-Pierre exclaimed. "What if they have developed a way to communicate telepathically, as your species does?"

Mariam thought for moment before answering. "It is possible they have developed new technology, however, they too have the ability to communicate telepathically through technology similar to that Frank uses. This could allow them to intercept our messages."

"It is a risk we must take grandfather."

"I agree." Sara said.

"I hope we aren't making a mistake." Jean-Pierre said.

Mariam focused her mind, concentrating on the caretakers. She wanted to focus all of her energy in order to maintain a direct link with them, hopefully at the same time, preventing the Dragonoids from intercepting her message.

"Come on, we will go inside, give her some space to work. I have to prepare my message as well." Sara said.

"Frank, can we talk while they do their parts?"

"Sure grandfather, why don't we go into the lab."

◆

Frank knew something was different about his grandfather, he could sense a change in him. A change for the better.

"You know Frank, since you arrived, things have been crazy here. There was a time in my life, a long – long time ago, that I believed in all of this faith talk. Then it all changed. The world began to change. People started to do things, they started to change. How could this be? I would ask myself that question. I would consider all the science, all the facts. Yet all of these things were happening in the world. I was missing something, what I was missing I did not know. Until now."

Jean-Pierre was silent as he thought about things.

"It is hard sometimes for people to have faith grandfather. When I was working along side the O.W.E. as Sims, I witnessed a lot of things. During that time, however, I was unaware of what I was truly seeing. I knew I had a mission and you were part of that mission, but I could not remember everything. There were things I still was unsure of, just as we have seen recently. As I slowly regained my memories I began to realize what was happening."

"I want to believe," Jean-Pierre said, "I really do. It is just – I am a scientist."

"There were many scientist throughout earth history who had faith in the Creator." Frank said, as he looked out a tiny window in the lab.

"I know."

"We need to focus on the current situation. I need you to focus and to believe. If these people see any doubt in your eyes, this entire mission could fail. Grandfather, please trust me. I am aware that our brief history has been less than perfect."

Jean-Pierre was silent. A look of despair shown on his face. He knew within his heart that Frank was right.

"Frank, I must apologize to you. I have doubted everything you have said. I have treated you as a spy. All of this time, you have been trying to help us, to help humanity as a whole."

"No need to apologize. You had every right to distrust me."

"Guys, we need to move now!" Sara shouted from within the other room.

Frank and Jean-Pierre quickly went to meet Sara. Her sudden shout was unsettling to them both, they knew something was wrong.

"Sara, what in the world is going on?" Jean-Pierre asked.

"I can explain," Mariam interjected. "I was able to contact the caretakers. We have a problem."

"The Dragonoids?" Frank questioned.

"Indeed. It appears they *are* up to something." Mariam said.

"Then we need to stop them!" Jean-Pierre exclaimed.

"It may not be that simple Dr. Valentine, sir."

"Mariam, you said you have access to other technology. Is it possible that you have something that could help us? A weapon of some type?"

"Frank, you know how we feel about that."

"I know, however, things have changed. I was chosen for this mission because of my human abilities. They knew that it could come to this."

"As you know Frank, violence is not our way. However, there may be a way, a less violent approach."

"No offense Mariam, but we know these beings apparently understand violence over peace. I have a mission to complete, and that is to save humanity. If that requires a more – violent approach, then, so-be-it."

Mariam was silent as she thought about what Frank was saying, she understood more than she let be known. She was aware that this could become more intense. Furthermore, Frank was right. This was going to take more than just – talking it out.

"Frank, you know I can never condone violence, and I understand what you are saying. Let me think about this--"

"Think about it?" Frank interrupted as he was beginning to feel more and more angry.

"Frank, please, allow me to work on something."

171

"Okay Mariam, I will allow you a short while, but then I am moving forward with my own plans. We must stop them before it is too late."

"Twenty-four hours, that is all I ask you. Give me that."

Mariam walked outside, taking in everything that Frank was saying, and everything that was happening. She knew something had to be done and done quickly if his mission was to be a success, however, she was bound by the non-violent nature of her people.

Back inside, Frank was also contemplating the situation and what could be done, to maintain a non-violent approach. He knew time was running out and he had to do something now.

"Frank," Mariam called from outside, "could you come here please?"

Making his way to join Mariam, Frank could since trouble.

"I know what we need to do," she began, "we need to move forward with the plan, but with a few additional changes. Changes that will involve you. And I am uncertain as to what it will actually involve. I only know that it is imperative that it takes place."

Mariam continued to inform Frank of the changes and he in turn told his grandparents. They were all uncertain, but one thing they all agreed on, was it had to be done. No matter what happens. There was more, but Mariam was unsure how to move forward or how much to reveal. She knew, no matter what, that Faizan and the Dragonoids had to be stopped.

Chapter Twenty-One
The End Is Near
Valentine Island, Earth, 2105

The wind off the Pacific carried a strange stillness, as if the world itself were holding its breath. Frank and Mariam stood at the edge of the cliff, overlooking the sea. The sky above them was streaked with auroras—an energy flowed, as if the universe knew what was about to take place, perhaps this was a part of the Creator's plan? It was beautiful. And ominous.

They had reached a decision, although not mutual. What they did agree on was simple: Faizan had to be stopped. But how —and at what cost—remained a major point of tension.

After a long silence, Mariam spoke. "Frank," she began slowly, "you – you were right. The technology I have access to does contain a weapon, of sorts. Not in the form you might expect to find."

Frank furled his brow. "I don't understand. If it's a weapon – but your people are non-violent."

"Indeed, my friend, we are. This weapon has the potential to destroy – or rebuild."

"Hold on," Frank interrupted. "Rebuild?"

Mariam nodded, her eyes reflecting the shimmer of the auroras. "I know this is confusing. But consider this: you've witnessed so much already. Time travel, alien beings, advanced technology. The *Beacon* is not a weapon in the traditional sense. It's a dimensional catalyst. It reflects what is brought to it – truth, fear, hope, or even destruction."

Frank stepped back, absorbing her words. "So if we activate it…"

"It will show humanity what it truly is. And what it could become."

They sat on a nearby rock, waves crashing below. Their conversation turned technical – quantum harmonics, bio-chip synchronization, Centaurian code sequences. But beneath the science was something much deeper: a reckoning.

"If we do this," Frank said, "we're not just exposing Faizan. We're exposing everything."

Mariam placed a hand on his shoulder. "That is the only way forward."

Back at the base, Jean-Pierre and Sara were preparing for the broadcast. The *Beacon*'s chamber had begun to respond to Frank's presence, as if it was meant to be. The tension among the group was palpable. They were preparing for the ultimate ending – or a new beginning.

As the sun dipped below the horizon, Frank stood alone for a moment, staring at the Moon.

"Are you ready?" Mariam asked, joining him.

He didn't answer. He simply turned toward the stars. Toward the Moon. Toward the future. He knew this had to be done, his only fear at the moment, was whether he was doing the right thing. Would this fix things, or make them worse?

"I need a moment," Frank said.

The others knew he needed a moment to pray, and left him to his thoughts and prayers. They knew, this was it, it was about to begin...

Chapter Twenty-Two

The Broadcast and the Betrayal

The Beacon's activation sequence required three keys: Frank's bio-chip, Mariam's Centaurian code, and a human signal of intent. Jean-Pierre hesitated.

"I've spent my life debunking faith, chasing the science and logic. But this – this is something else."

Sara placed her hand over his. "Then let's choose faith my love, together we can do this. With God, we can do this."

Together, they completed the sequence. The *Beacon* hummed with energy that filled the air like a living pulse. Frank paced, running a hand through his hair, while Mariam's fingers danced across the controls with precise calm.

"This is it," Mariam whispered, her eyes fixed on the flowing streams of data. "Once we start, there's no going back."

Frank paused, placing a steady hand on her shoulder. "Then we go. The world deserves the truth."

The wind carried an unnatural chill. Jean-Pierre stepped forward, his voice low and steady. "Do this with courage, Frank. Not for vengeance. Do this – so that history remembers."

Frank swallowed hard, feeling the weight of generations pressing on his shoulders. "I know. Let's give them the chance they deserve."

The hum shifted, and the One World Earth alert system began to pulse. Across the globe, millions of screens flickered, waiting for Faizan's commands. But instead of the tyrant's face, the beacon unfolded history – suppressed records, images of subverted leaders, manipulated events, and acts of heroism erased from memory.

Faizan's image erupted on the monitors, fury twisting his features. "Lies! Do not believe them!"

Mariam's voice carried through the air, calm but firm. "I've got this." With a wave of her hand, she activated a counter-signal. The technology pulsed, and Faizan's broadcast fractured, looping back on itself until it fell silent, leaving only a gentle hum in the air.

Frank stepped forward into the projection. His voice carried across the globe, steady, unwavering:

"Humanity was never weak. You were made to choose, to build, to rise. You were create for a purpose. Do not surrender that gift again."

The Beacon, now roaring with life, sending a pulse through the air, into Earth's atmosphere. Across the globe, screens flickered. Faizan's broadcasts now fully overridden. The truth spilled out into the airways – alien manipulation, the Dragonoid agenda, the Centaurian alliance, and Frank's origin.

But in the shadows of the base, a figure was moving. Commander Rourke – once loyal to Faizan – had infiltrated the base. He aimed a rifle at the Beacon's core.

"You think you're saving humanity," he snarled. "You're handing it over to the aliens!"

Frank stepped between him and the Beacon. "No! We're giving humanity a choice. You must trust us. Please!"

Rourke fired.

Frank's bio-chip flared, absorbing the blast. He collapsed, but the *Beacon* held.

Mariam rushed to his side. "He's not gone," she said as she glanced towards Jean-Pierre. "He's becoming what he is meant to be."

The *Beacon* pulsed again – this time brighter, deeper. A new wormhole formed, swirling with energy and bright auroras as Frank's body lifted into the newly formed portal. A blinding light pierced through the air.

Jean-Pierre stared as he shielded his eyes. "Is that – Frank?"

Mariam nodded. "Or what he left behind. Do not be afraid doctor, your grandson's sacrifice will be this world's redemption."

Sara fought back tears: "Is he – dead?"

"Honestly, I cannot answer that question. Dead? I am not sure. Alive? In a sense, I would say, yes."

"When will we know?" Asked Jean-Pierre.

"It could be immediate, or it could be days. Even weeks. One thing is for certain doctor, a change has taken place. I can feel it. It is almost – peaceful, in a way."

Mariam walked slowly to the *Beacon* now sitting silent and powerless. She knew a change had taken place, but she could no longer sense the presence of the guardians. Were they still there, in their Lunar base? Had they too left? The connection was gone, for now at least.

At least a week would pass before the Valentines would know for sure if this worked. In the meantime, Mariam would stay on the island with them. Waiting and watching, to see what changes would take place – if any.

◆

Earth didn't change overnight – but it felt like it had.

In the days following the *Beacon's* activation, the skies over major cities shimmered with residual energy. Power grids stabilized. Communication networks, once tightly controlled by Faizan's regime, became open channels of truth. The Dragonoid threat was exposed, and their cloaked ships retreated beyond lunar orbit, their plans disrupted.

Jean-Pierre stood before a crowd in Geneva, no longer a skeptic but now, a symbol of transformation. "We were blind," he said, as his voice trembled. "Not because we lacked science – but because we lacked courage to believe in something greater than ourselves. We needed an awakening, a spiritual awakening."

Sara watched from the sidelines, her fingers wrapped around a small pendant that Jean-Pierre made her, from a fragment of the bio-chip Frank had left behind. It pulsed faintly, almost like a heartbeat.

Mariam returned to Centaur, but not in silence. Her final transmission to Earth was broadcast globally:

"You have awakened. But awakening is not the end – it is the beginning. The Wormhole remains open. How you choose to see it or use it will define your legacy. A path awaits you, that can help you to rebuild. It is now up to you. Will you choose faith or fear? Power or spiritual strength?"

Governments scrambled to respond. Some called for unity. Others feared more alien manipulation. A new council formed – The Accord – led by scientists, philosophers, and spiritual leaders. Jean-Pierre was appointed as its first chair.

But beneath the optimism, whispers began to spread. Tales of children dreaming of Frank. Machines responding to unknown signals. A frequency embedded in the remnant of the *Beacon's* pulse – one that hadn't been there before. Now humming with a new-found power. A power that seemed to come from the people of earth. A sign of hope and strength. The days would surely be hard, as they began to rebuild.

A group of Centaurians had came through the wormhole, not to stay, but to cleanse. Taking with them Faizan and his remaining regime. Forcing the remainder of the Dragonoids through a portal, back to their space. With a warning, to never return. A new day was upon the earth. A new life awaits those who will embrace the changes. Will there be peace on earth at last? Will eyes finally be opened to the truth and will faith rise above fear? These are questions that can only be answered with time. Before leaving, a Centaurian guard turned to Jean-Pierre...

"Doctor Valentine, your grandson has made it possible now for blinded eyes to be opened. We do not know what the Creator holds for your immediate future. We know that change is in the air, a change that could take place at once or over a period of time. All we can say is this. Hold to the faith that you now understand more."

With that, they left. Leaving behind a new, yet, still torn world. Needing new leadership and a rebirth.

Chapter Twenty-Three
The Signal and the Seed

In a quiet lab beneath the Andes, a young prodigy named Elian decoded the *Beacon's* residual frequency. It wasn't random. It was structured. Intentional.

He played it aloud.

A voice emerged – fractured, distant, but unmistakably human.

"If you're hearing this… I made it. Not as I was – but as I became."

Jean-Pierre listened in stunned silence. "Frank?"

Sara nodded. "Or, what's left of him."

The signal contained coordinates – deep space, near Alpha Centauri. A new anomaly. A second Wormhole. But this one wasn't created by Earth or Centaurian tech. It was older. Organic. Possibly sentient.

The Accord debated next steps. Should humanity send a ship? Maybe a probe? Or, should they do nothing at all?

Jean-Pierre stood once again before the council. "We as a species have spent centuries fearing the unknown. My son and his team did not. They ventured through space, finding hope for humanity, and that hope came in my grandson Frank. He stepped forward, into a wormhole from a distant galaxy, traveling through space and time. Maybe it's time we follow in their footsteps."

Jean-Pierre and Sara volunteered to lead the mission. Elian, the new-found prodigy, joined them. Mariam, who had recently resumed communications with earth via the now stable wormhole agreed to send a Centaurian vessel, retrofitted for human travel.

The crew began preparations for their departure. Following the guidance of Mariam from far-away. As the ship launched, the world watched. Not with fear – but with hope.

And far beyond the stars, something – or someone, watched back. What would be waiting? A new species or a new threat? Or was it something more? There is so much that awaits and so much that could go wrong. Yet there is also a lot that can be positive in that which awaits.

Epilogue – The Whispering Guide

The wormhole shimmered at the edge of known space, its spiraling currents twisting with colors no spectrum could explain. It hung there like a wound in the stars—fragile, infinite, and impossible to ignore. A new mission was starting. A new and unknown adventure awaits.

The Valentines had their orders as they departed into the unknown. Their ship cut a steady line toward the anomaly, it's mission both daring and uncertain. Humanity watched with held breath, aware that what waited on the other side could reshape everything they understood; about life, time, and the multiverse itself.

From the observation deck the newly formed mission team watched, as a new Beacon, created just for this mission, shone against the dark; its glow steady and unwavering, lighting the way. To most it was a monument, a silent guardian. But to the others, especially Sara, who was staring at the restless swirl of the wormhole, felt something more. In the Beacon's rhythm there was a presence—faint but familiar, patient, and guiding.

Not a voice. Not a sound. A thread of intention, woven into thought.

Deep within the Beacon's living lattice of light and energy, Frank endured. Not gone. Not forgotten. Watching. Waiting.

As the Valentines crossed the threshold, the wormhole pulsed with resonance, as though answering a call, a calling that humanity had only just begun to hear. Where will it lead? What will they find along the way? What lies ahead, or – behind?

In Loving Memory:

It has been a long process in completing this project. If it had not been for the support of my family, I would not be who I am.

I hereby dedicate this book to the loving memory of my parents: Dennis Lee Bates Sr & Mildred Diane Bates

We love you and we miss you, Cody and I will be okay, but we will always miss you in our daily lives.

We know that Daddy (Paw Paw) is fishing on the river side, and Momma (Maw Maw) is chasing those butterflies.

Fly High – We Love You!!

Made in the USA
Columbia, SC
20 December 2025

76544571R00104